I FOLLOWED MARCIA TO HER ROOM . . .

She pushed her door open and groped for the light switch.

When the lights went on I heard her gasp. She was standing as if frozen, her back to me, her hands up to her throat.

Then she screamed, a high, tearing scream.

"The murderer. Oh my God, the murderer. . . ."

She grabbed my arm and pointed to the bed, her lips shaking so much that she couldn't speak coherently.

I stared down at the bed, while the slow goose flesh pricked up my spine.

Lying on the coverlet was a doll, the kind of frivolous doll I had seen dozens of times.

But this one was different.

It was lying flat on its back on the bed, with its legs straight out and its hands crossed on its breast. The contents of an ash tray had been scattered over it, and a great red gash gleamed across its neck, where its throat was cut from ear to ear. . . .

Fawcett Crest Books
by Mary Stewart:

Airs Above The Ground

The Gabriel Hounds

The Ivy Tree

Madam, Will You Talk?

The Moon-Spinners

My Brother Michael

Nine Coaches Waiting

This Rough Magic

Thunder on the Right

Touch Not the Cat

A Walk in Wolf Wood

Wildfire at Midnight

THE MERLIN NOVELS

The Crystal Cave

The Hollow Hills

The Last Enchantment

The Wicked Day

WILDFIRE
AT
MIDNIGHT

by Mary Stewart

FAWCETT CREST • NEW YORK

To F. H. S.

"Wildfire at midnight. In this heedless fury
He may show violence to cross himself.
I'll follow the event."

Tourneur: *The Revenger's Tragedy*

Chapter 1

IN THE FIRST PLACE, I suppose, it was my parents' fault for giving me a silly name like Gianetta. It is a pretty enough name in itself, but it conjures up pictures of delectable and slightly overblown ladies in Titan's less respectable canvases, and, though I admit I have the sort of coloring that might have interested that Venetian master, I happen to be the rather inhibited product of an English country rectory. And if there is anything further removed than that from the *bagnio* Venuses of Titian's middle period, I don't know what it is.

To do my parents justice, I must confess straightaway that the *bagnio* touch was there in the family—nicely in the past, of course, but known nevertheless to be there. And my mother is just sufficiently vague, artistic, and sentimental to see nothing against calling a red-haired daughter after the Vixen Venus, the lovely redheaded Gianetta Fox, who was once the rage of London, and a Beauty in the days when beauties had a capital B, and were moreover apt to regard beauty and capital as one and the same thing. She was a nobody, the lovely Gianetta; her mother, I believe, was half Italian, and if she knew who her father was, she never admitted to him. She simply appeared, Venus rising from the scum of Victorian Whitechapel, and hit London for six in the spring of 1858. She was just seventeen. By the time she was twenty she had been painted by every painter who mattered (Landseer was the only abstainer), in every conceivable allegorical pose, and had also, it was said, been the mistress of every one of them in turn—I should be inclined here, too, to give Landseer the benefit of the doubt. And in 1861 she reaped the due reward of her peculiar virtues and married a baronet. He managed to keep her long enough to beget two children of her before she left him—for a very "modern" painter of the French school who specialized in nudes. She left her son and daughter behind in Sir Charles's scandalized care; the former was to be my maternal grandfather.

So my nice, vague, artistic mother, who spends her time in our Cotswold rectory making dear little pots and bowls and baking them in a kiln at the bottom of the garden, called me after my disreputable (and famous) great-grandmother, without a thought about the possible consequences to me when I hit London in my turn, in 1945.

I was nineteen, had left school a short eight months before, and now, fresh from a West End training course for mannequins, was ingenuously setting out on a glamorous career with a fashion house, modeling clothes. I had a share in a bed-sitting room, a small banking account (gift from Father), two hand-thrown pots and an ash tray (gift from Mother), and an engagement diary (gift from my brother Lucius). I was on top of the world.

I was still on top of the world when the Morelli Gallery acquired the Zollner canvas called "My Lady Greensleeves," and Marco Morelli—*the* Marco Morelli—decided to make a splash with it. You remember the fuss, perhaps? Morelli's idea was, I think, to stage a sort of comeback of art after the austerities and deprivations of the war. He could hardly have chosen a more appropriate picture to do it with. "My Lady Greensleeves" has all the rioting bravura of Zollner's 1860 period: the gorgeous lady who languishes, life-size, in the center of the canvas is the focus of a complicated shimmer of jewels and feathers and embroidered silk—I doubt if any material has ever been more miraculously painted than the coruscating damask of the big green sleeves. As an antidote to austerity it was certainly telling. And even Zollner's peacock riot of color could not defeat his model's triumphant vitality, or drain the fire from that flaming hair. It was Gianetta Fox's last full-dress appearance in canvas, and she had all the air of making the most of it.

So had Morelli, and his cousin Hugo Montefior, the dress designer, who happened to be my employer. And there really was nothing against the idea that Montefior should re-create the dress with the lovely green sleeves, and that I should wear it at the showing, and that there should be a sensation in the right circles, thereby doing the cousins a lot of good. And, possibly, me too, though this honestly didn't occur to me when Hugo put his idea in front of me. I was merely flattered, excited, and terribly nervous.

So I wore the Greensleeves gown at the show, and Morelli got his sensation, and I was so scared of the fashionable crowd that when I spoke at all, it was in a tight, flat little voice that must have sounded the last word in bored, brittle sophistication. I must have looked and sounded, in fact, like a pale copy of that arrogant worldling behind me in Zollner's canvas, for that is what Nicholas Drury undoubtedly took me for, when at length he elbowed his way through the crowds and introduced himself. I had heard of him, of course, and this in no way increased my self-confidence: He had at that time—he was twenty-nine—three terrifyingly good novels to his credit, as well as a reputation for a scarifying tongue. I, for one, was so thoroughly scarified that I froze into complete stupidity, and under his sardonic look stammered some meaningless schoolgirl rubbish that, God help us both, he took for coquetry. We were married three months later.

I have no wish to dwell on the three years that followed. I was wildly, madly, dumbly in love with him, of course, a silly little star-dazzled adolescent, plunged into a life completely strange and rather terrifying. And Nicholas, it became very quickly apparent, wasn't on his own ground either. What he had meant to marry was a modern Gianetta Fox, a composed young sophisticate who could hold her own in the fast-moving society to which he was accustomed; what he'd actually got was only Gianetta Brooke, not long out of school, whose poise was a technique very recently acquired in Montefior's salons and the Mayfair mannequin factory.

Not that this initial miscasting was the cause of our little tragedy; love is a great builder of bridges, and it did seem at first as though what was between us could have spanned any gap. And Nicholas tried as hard as I. Looking back now, I can see that; if I did achieve sophistication, and a little wisdom, Nicholas struggled to rediscover tenderness. But it was too late; already, when we met, it was too late. The times were out of joint for us, the gap too wide—not the ten years' gap between our ages, but the thousand-year-long stretch of a world war that to me was only an adolescent memory hardly denting the surface of my life, but to Nicholas was a still-recurring nightmare agony leaving scars on the mind which were then only precariously skinning over. How was I, untouched nineteen, to apprehend the sort of stresses that drove

Nicholas? And how was he to guess that, deep down under my precarious self-confidence, lurked the destroying germs of insecurity and fear?

Whatever the causes, the break came soon enough. In two years the marriage was as good as over. When Nicholas traveled, as he often did, in search of material for his books, he more and more frequently found reasons for not taking me with him, and when at length I found he was not traveling alone, I felt no surprise, but I was hurt and humiliated, and so—I have red hair, after all—blazingly outspoken.

If I had wanted to keep Nicholas, I should have done better to have held my tongue. I was no match for him on a battlefield where love had become a weakness and pride the only defense against a cynicism both brutal and unanswerable. He won very easily, and he cannot have known how cruelly. . . .

We were divorced in 1949. For the sake of my mother, who is so High Church as to be verging (according to Father), on Popish Practices, I kept Nicholas's name, and I still wore my wedding ring. I even, after a time, went back to London and to Hugo Montefior, who was angelically kind to me, worked me to death, and never once mentioned Nicholas. Nor did anyone else, except Mother, who occasionally asked after him in her letters, and even, on two occasions, wondered if we were thinking of starting a family. . . . After a year or so I even managed to find this amusing, except when I was run-down and tired, and then the gentle timelessness of Mother and Tench Abbas Rectory became more than I could bear.

So in mid-May last year, when London had been packed to suffocation for weeks with the Coronation crowds already massing for the great day, and Hugo Montefior one morning took a long look at my face, took another, and promptly told me to go away for a fortnight, I rang up Tench Abbas, and got Mother.

"A holiday?" said Mother. "The beginning of June? How lovely, darling. Are you coming down here, or will Nicholas find it too dull?"

"Mother, I—"

"Of course we haven't got television," said Mother proudly, "but we can listen to the *whole thing* on the wireless. . . ."

I spared a glance for Montefior's salon windows, which have a grandstand view of Regent Street. "That would be lovely," I said. "But, Mother dearest, would you mind if I went somewhere else for a bit first? Somewhere away from everything . . . you know, just hills and water and birds and things. I'd thought of the Lake District."

"Not far enough," said Mother promptly. "Skye."

Knowing Mother, I thought for one wild moment that she was recommending heaven as suitably remote. But then she added: "Your father was talking about it at the Dunhills' garden party the other day. It rained *all* the time, you know, and so we had to be indoors—you know how it *always* rains for the Dunhills' garden party, darling?— well, it did so *remind* Maisie Dunhill. They were there a fortnight once, and it rained *every day*."

"Oh," I said, as light dawned. "Skye."

"And," said Mother, clinching it, "there's *no television*."

"It sounds the very place," I said, without irony. "Did Mrs. D. give you an address?"

"There are the pips," said Mother distractedly. "We *can't* have had three minutes, and they *know* how it puts me off. What was—oh, yes, the Dunhills . . . do you know, darling, they've bought a new car, a *huge* thing, called a Jackal or a Jaeger or something, and—"

"Jaguar, Mother. But you were going to give me the address of the hotel where the Dunhills stayed."

"Oh yes, that was it. But you know Colonel Dunhill *never* drives at more than thirty-five miles an hour, and your father says—what, dear?"

I heard Father's voice speaking indistinguishably somewhere beyond her. Then she said: "Your father has it, dear, written down. I don't quite know how . . . well, here it is. The Camas Fhionnaridh Hotel—"

"The *what* hotel, Mother?"

"Camas—I'll spell it." She did. "I really don't think—I don't remember—but this *must* be the one. What did you say, dear?" This to Father again, as she turned away from the receiver, leaving me listening in some apprehension for the pips, which always reduce Mother from her normal pleasant abstraction to a state of gibbering incoherence. "Your father says it's Gaelic and pronounced Camasunary," said Mother, "and it's at the back of *beyond,* so you go there, darling, and have a lovely time with the birds and the—the water, or whatever you said you wanted."

I sat clutching the receiver, perched there above the roar of Regent Street. Before my mind's eye rose, cool and remote, a vision of rain-washed mountains.

"D'you know," I said slowly, "I think I will."

"Then that's settled," said Mother comfortably. "It sounds the very thing, darling. So *handy* having that address. It's as if it were *meant*."

I am glad to think that Mother will never appreciate the full irony of that remark.

So it came about that, in the late afternoon of Saturday, May 30th, 1953, I found myself setting out on the last stage of my journey to Camas Fhionnaridh in the Isle of Skye. Mother, I found, had been right enough about the back of beyond. The last stage had to be undertaken by boat, there being only a rough cart road overland from Strathaird to Camas Fhionnaridh, which the solitary local bus would not tackle. This same bus had brought me as far as Elgol, on the east side of Loch Scavaig, and had more or less dumped me and my cases on the shore. And presently a boatman, rather more ceremoniously, dumped me into his boat, and set out with me, my cases, and one other passenger, across the shining sea loch towards the distant bay of Camasunary.

Nothing could have been more peaceful. The sea loch itself was one huge bay, an inlet of the Atlantic, cradled in the crescent of the mountains. The fishing village of Elgol, backed by its own heather hills, was within one tip of the crescent; from the other soared sheer from the sea a jagged wall of mountains, purple against the sunset sky. The Cuillin, the giants of the Isle of Mist.

And, locked in the great arms of the mountains, the water lay quiet as a burnished shield, reflecting in deeper blue and deeper gold the pageantry of hill and sky. One thin gleaming line, bright as a rapier, quivered between the world of reality and the water-world below. Our boat edged its way, with drowsily purring engine, along the near shore of the loch. Water lipped softly under the bows and whispered along her sides. The tide was at half ebb, its gentle washes dwindling, one after one, among the sea tangle at its edge. The seaweeds, black and rose-red and olive-green, rocked as the salt swell took them, and the smell of the sea drifted up, sharp and exciting. The shore slid past; scree and heather, overhung with summer clouds of birch, flowed by us, and our wake arrowed the silk-smooth water into ripples of copper and indigo.

And now ahead of us, in the center of the mountain

crescent, I could see the dip of a bay, where a green valley cut through the hills to the sea's edge. Higher up this valley, as I knew, was a loch, where the hills crowded in and cradled the water into a deep and narrow basin. Out of this the river flowed; I could see the gleam of it, and, just discernible at that distance, a white building set among a mist of birch trees where the glittering shallows fanned out to meet the sea. The boat throbbed steadily closer. Now I could see the smoke from the hotel chimneys, a faint penciling against the darker blue of the hills. Then the glitter of water vanished as the sun slipped lower, and the enormous shadow of the Cuillin strode across the little valley. One arrogant wing of rock, thrusting itself across the sun, flung a diagonal of shadow over half the bay.

"Garsven," said the other passenger, at my elbow. I jumped. Such had been my absorption in the scene, so great the sense of solitude imposed by these awful hills, that I had forgotten I was not alone.

"I beg your pardon?"

He smiled. I saw now that he was a pleasant-looking man of perhaps thirty, with hair of an unusual dark gold color, and very blue eyes. He was tall and lightly built, but he looked strong and wiry, and his face was tanned as if he spent most of his time in the open. He was wearing an ancient ulster over what had, once, been very good tweeds. "This must be your first visit," he said.

"It is. It's a little—overpowering, wouldn't you say?"

He laughed. "Decidedly. I know the district like the back of my hand, but they still take my breath away, every time."

"They?"

"The Cuillin." He gave the word what I imagined must be its local pronunciation. His gaze had moved beyond me, and I turned to follow it. "Garsven," he said again. "That's the one at the end that sweeps straight up out of the sea at that impossible angle." His hand came over my shoulder, pointing. "And that's Sgurr nan Eag; then the big one blotting out the sun—that's the Pointed Peak, Sgurr Biorach."

"You mean Sgurr Alasdair," put in the boatman unexpectedly from behind us. He was a sturdy Skye man with a dark square face and the soft voice of the Islands. He steered the boat nonchalantly, and now and then spat to leeward. "Sgurr Alasdair," he said again.

The fair man grinned, and said something in Gaelic which brought an answering grin to the boatman's face. Then he said to me: "Murdo's right, of course. It's Alasdair on the maps—it was rechristened after some mountaineer or other; but I like the old names best. Sgurr Biorach it is, and that next to it is Sgurr Dearg, the Red Peak." His pointing finger swung towards the last towering pinnacle, black against the sunset. "Sgurr nan Gillean." He dropped his hand and gave me the sort of smile that holds the hint of an apology—the Britisher's regret for having displayed an emotion. He said lightly: "And you couldn't have had your first sight of them under better conditions. Sunset and evening star—all the works, in fact, in glorious Technicolor."

"You must be a mountaineer," I said.

"A climber? Yes, of a sort."

"He's a good man on the hill, is Mr. Grant," said Murdo.

Grant took out cigarettes, offered them to me and Murdo, then spun a spent match into the water. He said to me: "Have you come for long?"

"A week or ten days. It depends on the weather. If it stays like this, it'll be heaven."

"It won't," he said confidently. "What d'you say, Murdo?"

The boatman cast a dubious eye at the southwest, where the Atlantic merged its long and glimmering reaches into a deep blue sky. He jerked a thumb in that direction, and spoke briefly and to the point. "Rain," he said.

"Oh dear." I was dismayed. This golden prospect seemed, now that I was here, to be infinitely more desirable than the rain-washed hills of my dreams.

"Never mind," said Mr. Grant cheerfully, "it'll improve the fishing." I must have looked blank, because he added: "You do fish, of course?"

"Oh no." To my own surprise I sounded apologetic. "But I—I could learn."

His interest quickened. "You climb, then?"

"No." I felt suddenly very urban and tripperish. "Actually I came for a—a rest, and quiet. That's all."

His eye fell on my cases. "London?" He grinned. "Well, you've certainly come to the right place if you want to get out of the crowds. You'll have no neighbors except the Black Cuillin, and the nearest of them is—" He stopped abruptly.

"Nearest?" I glanced at the hotel, much closer now, is-landed in its green valley, dwarfed and overborne by one great solitary mountain to the east. "That mountain? Is that one of them too? You didn't speak of it before. What's it called?"

He hesitated perceptibly. "That's Blaven."

The boatman took his cigarette from his mouth, and spat into the water. "Blah-ven," he repeated, in his soft Highland voice. "Mph—mm. . . ."

"The Blue Mountain . . ." said Grant in a voice that was almost abstracted. Then he pitched his cigarette into the water, and said abruptly: "Was London so very crowded?"

"Oh yes. It's been steadily filling up with people and excitement for months. Now it's like a great pot slowly simmering to boiling point."

Murdo turned the boat's nose neatly towards the river mouth. "London, is it?" His voice held a naïve note of wonder. "Did ye not want to stay and see the Coronation, mistress?"

"In a way, I did. But I—I've been a bit overworked, so I thought a holiday was a better idea after all."

"What made you come here?" asked Grant. His eyes were still on the Blue Mountain.

"To Skye? Oh, I don't know—everybody wants to visit Skye at some time or other, don't they? And I wanted quiet and a complete change. I shall go for long walks in the hills."

"Alone?" There was something in Murdo's expression that made me stare at him.

"Why, yes," I said in surprise.

I saw his eyes meet Grant's for a moment, then slide away to watch the approaching jetty. I laughed. "I shan't get lost," I said. "The walks won't be long enough for that—don't forget I'm a city bird. I don't suppose I'll get farther than the loch, or the lower slopes of—Blaven, was it? Nothing much can happen to me there!" I turned to Mr. Grant. "Does Murdo think I'll go astray in the mist, or run off with a water kelpie?" Then I stopped. His eyes, meeting mine, held some indefinable expression, the merest shadow, no more, but I hesitated, aware of some obscure uneasiness.

The blue eyes dropped. "I imagine Murdo means—"

But Murdo cut the engine, and the sudden silence interrupted as effectively as an explosion. "London . . ." said Murdo meditatively into the bowls of his engine. "That's a long way now! A long way, indeed, to come. . . ." The guileless wonder was back in his voice, but I got the embarrassing impression that he was talking entirely at random. And, moreover, that his air of Highland simplicity was a trifle overdone; he had, I judged, a reasonably sophisticated eye. "A very fine city, so they say. Westminster Abbey, Piccadilly Circus, the Zoo. I have seen pictures—"

"Murdo," I said suspiciously, as we bumped gently alongside a jetty, and made fast. "When did *you* last see London?"

He met my eye with a limpid gaze as he handed me out of the boat. "Eight years ago, mistress," he said in his soft voice, "on my way back frae Burma and points East. . . ."

The man called Grant had picked up my cases and had started walking up the path to the hotel. As I followed him I was conscious of Murdo staring after us for a long moment, before he turned back to his boat. That simple Skyeman act had been—what? Some kind of smoke screen? But what had there been to hide? Why had he been so anxious to change the conversation?

The path skirted the hotel to the front door, which faced the valley. As I followed my guide round the corner of the building my eye was once again, irresistibly, drawn to the great lonely bulk of the mountain in the east, stooping over the valley like a hawk.

Blaven? The Blue Mountain?

I turned my back on it and went into the hotel.

Chapter 2

IT WAS AN HOUR LATER. I had washed, brushed the railway smoke out of my hair, and changed. I sat in the hotel lounge, enjoying a moment of solitude before the other guests assembled for dinner. I was sipping an excellent sherry, my feet were in front of a pleasant fire, and on three sides of the lounge the tremendous mountain scenery was mine for the gazing. I felt good.

The door of the hotel porch swung and clashed, and presently, through the glass of the lounge doors, I saw two women come into the hall and cross it towards the stairs. One I judged to be about my own age; she was shortish, dark, thickset, with her hair cropped straight and mannishly, and the climber's uniform of slacks, boots, and heavy jersey exaggerated her masculine appearance. The other was a girl of about twenty, very young-looking, with bright red cheeks and straight black hair. She did not, I thought, look particularly happy, and her shoulders strained forward under her rucksack as if she were tired. The pair of them stumped up the first flight of the stairs and round the corner.

In a minute or so they were followed by an elderly couple, both tall, thin, and a little stooping, with gentle well-bred faces and deplorable hats. They solemnly carried an empty fishing creel between them up the stairs, and on their heels another woman trudged, hands thrust deep into the pockets of an ulster. I couldn't see her face, but her hunched shoulders and lifeless step told their own story of depression or weariness.

I yawned and stretched a toe to the blaze, and drank some more sherry. Idly I turned the pages of an old society weekly which lay at my elbow. The usual flashlighted faces, cruelly caught at hunt suppers and charity balls, gaped from the glossy pages ... beautiful horses, plain women, well-dressed men ... the *London Telephone Directory*, I thought, would be far more interesting. I flicked the pages. There was the usual photograph of me, this time poised against an Adam mantelpiece, in one of Hugo Montefior's most inspired evening gowns ... I remembered it well, a lovely frock. Here was the theatre page—Alec Guinness in an improbable beard, Vivien Leigh making every other woman within reach look plain, Marcia Maling giving the camera the famous three-cornered smile, staring at vacancy with those amazing eyes. ...

The lounge door swung open and whooshed shut with a breathless little noise. Marcia Maling came in, sat down opposite me, and rang for a drink.

I blinked at her. There was no mistake. That smooth

honey-gold hair, the wide lovely eyes, the patrician little
nose and the by-no-means patrician mouth—this was certainly the star of that string of romantic successes that had
filled one of London's biggest theatres from the first years
of the war, and was still packing it today.

The drink came. Marcia Maling took it, tasted it, met
my eyes across it and smiled, perfunctorily. Then the smile
slid into a stare.

"Forgive me"—it was the familiar husky voice—"but
haven't we met? I know you, surely?"

I smiled. "It's very brave of you to say so, Miss Maling.
I imagine you usually have to dodge people who claim
they've met you. But no, we've never met."

"I've seen you before, I'm sure."

I flicked the pages of the magazine with a fingernail.
"Probably. I model clothes."

Recognition dawned. "So you do! Then *that's* where!
You model for Montefior, don't you?"

"More often than not—though I do a bit of free-lancing
too. My name's Drury. Gianetta Drury. I know yours, of
course. And of course I saw your show, *and* the one before,
and the one before that—"

"Back to the dawn of time, my dear. I know. But how
nice of you. You must have been in pigtails when we did
Wild Belles."

I laughed. "I cut them off early. I had a living to earn."

"And how." Marcia drank gin, considering me. "But I
remember where I saw you now. It wasn't in a photograph;
it was at Leducq's winter show last year. I bought that
divine cocktail frock—"

"The topaz velvet. I remember it. It was a heavenly
dress."

She made a face over her glass. "I suppose so. But a mistake for all that. You know as well as I do that it wasn't
built for a blonde."

"You weren't a blonde when you bought it," I said,
fairly, before I thought. "Sorry," I added hastily, "I—"

But she laughed, a lovely joyous gurgle of sound. "Neither was I. I'd forgotten. I'd gone auburn for *Mitzi.* It
didn't suit me, and *Mitzi* was a flop anyway." She stretched
her exquisite legs in front of her and gave me the famous
three-cornered smile. "I'm so glad you've come. I've only
been here three days and I'm homesick already for town.
This is the first time since I left that I've even been able to

think about civilized things like clothes, and I do so adore them, don't you?"

"Of course. But as they're my job—"

"I know," she said. "But nobody here talks about *anything* but fishing or climbing, and I think they're too utterly dreary."

"Then what on earth are you doing here?" The question was involuntary, and too abrupt for politeness, but she answered without resentment.

"My dear. Resting."

"Oh, I see." I tried to sound noncommittal, but Marcia Maling lifted an eyebrow at me and laughed again.

"No," she said, "I mean it; really resting—not just out of a job. The show came off a week ago. Adrian said I positively *must vegetate,* and I had just read a divine book on Skye, so here I am."

"And doesn't Skye come up to the book?"

"In a way. The hills are quite terribly pretty and all that, and I saw some deer yesterday with the cutest baby, but the trouble is you can't really get around. Do you like walking—*rough* walking?"

"I do, rather."

"Well, I don't. And Fergus just simply refuses to take the car over some of these roads."

"Fergus? You're here with your husband, then?" I tried vainly to remember who was Marcia Maling's current man.

"My *dear!* I'm not married *at all,* just now. Isn't it heaven, for a change?" She gave a delicious little chuckle over her pink gin, and I found myself smiling back. Her charm was a tangible thing, something radiant and richly alive, investing her silliest clichés and her outdated extravagances of speech with a heart-warming quality that was as real as the blazing fire between us. "No. Fergus is my chauffeur."

"Marcia!" The name was out before I realized it; the fact that I used it was, in a way, a tribute to that charm. "You haven't brought a *car and chauffeur* here? Is that what you call vegetating?"

"Well, I hate walking," she said reasonably, "and anyway, we're not staying here all the time. I'm on a sort of tour of the Highlands and Islands. Let's have another drink. No, really, it's on me." She reached out and pressed the bell. "In a way, we came here because of Fergus. He

was born here. Not that he cares much for auld lang syne
and all that, but it seemed as good a place as any to come
to."

I stared at her. I couldn't help it. "You're very—consid-
erate," I said. "Your employees—"

She looked at me. This time the famous smile was definitely the one from that very naughty show *Yes, My
Darling*. "Aren't I just? But Fergus—oh, a dry sherry,
isn't it? And another pink gin." She gave the order and
turned back to me. "D'you know, if I talked like this to
anyone else in the hotel they'd freeze like—like stuffed
trout."

"Who else is in the hotel?"

"Well, let's see. . . . There's Colonel and Mrs. Cowdray-
Simpson. They're dim, but rather sweet. They fish all the
time, day and night, and have never, to my certain knowledge, caught anything at all."

"I think I saw them come in. Elderly, with an empty
creel?"

"That's them all right. Then, still talking of fish, there's
Mr. and Mrs. Corrigan and Mr. Braine."

"Not Alastair Braine, by any odd chance?"

"I believe that is his name." Her glance was speculative.
"A friend of yours?"

"I've met him. He's in advertising."

"Well, he's with this Corrigan couple. And," added
Marcia meditatively, "if ever I could find it in me to pity
a woman who's married to a man as good-looking as
Hartley Corrigan, I'd pity that one."

"Why?" I asked, amused. Marcia Maling's views on
marriage, delivered personally, ought to be worth listening
to.

"Fish," she said, simply.

"Fish? Oh, I get it. You mean *fish?*"

"Exactly. He and Alastair Braine, they're just like the
Cowdray-Simpsons. Morning, noon, and night. *Fish.* And
she does nothing—*nothing*—to fight it, though she's obviously having an utterly foul time, and has been for weeks.
She moons miserably about alone with her hands in her
pockets."

I remembered the depressed-looking woman who had
trudged upstairs in the wake of the Cowdray-Simpsons. "I
think I've seen her. She didn't look too happy, I agree.
But I doubt," I said thoughtfully, "if there's a woman

living who could compete with fish, once they've really got hold of a man."

Marcia Maling wriggled her lovely body deeper into her chair, and said: "No?"

"All right," I said. "You, possibly. Or Rita Hayworth. But no lesser woman."

"But she doesn't even *try!*" said Marcia indignantly. "And he—oh well, who else?"

"I saw two women—" I began.

"Oh yes, the—what's the word?—*schwärmerinen,*" said Marcia, in her lovely, carrying voice. "They—"

"Marcia, *no!* You really musn't!"

But the crusading spirit seemed to be unexpectedly strong in Miss Maling. Her fine eyes flashed. "That child!" she exclaimed. "Nineteen if she's a day, and dragged everywhere by that impossible female with the mustache! My dear, she bullies her, positively!"

"If she didn't like the female," I said reasonably, "why would she come with her?"

"I told you. They're—"

"*No,* Marcia. It's slander, or something. Do remember this is a Scottish fishing hotel, not a theatre cocktail party."

"I suppose you're right." She sighed. "Actually, they come from the same school, or something. The little one's just started teaching there, and the other one takes P.K. or R.T. or something. I heard her actually *admitting* it."

"Admitting what?" I asked, startled.

"Teaching this R.T. or whatever it is. What is it?"

"Muscular Christianity, I should think."

"Well, there you are," said Marcia gloomily.

"Who else is there? I met a man in the boat coming over from Elgol—"

"That would be Roderick Grant. He practically *lives* here, I believe. Tallish, nice-looking, with rather gorgeous hair?"

"That's the one. Blue eyes."

"And how," said Marcia, with feeling. "He's *definitely* interesting, that is, if it wasn't for—" She broke off and drank some gin.

Conscious of a steadily mounting curiosity to see Fergus, I said merely: "I gathered that this Roderick Grant is a fisherman too."

"What? Oh, yes, they all are," said Marcia bitterly. "But I must say, he's only spasmodic about it. Most of the time he walks, or something. He's never in the hotel."

"He's a climber," I said, amused.

"Probably. There's another climber chap called Beagle."

"Ronald Beagle?"

"I believe so. Another friend of yours?"

"No. I've never met him, but I've heard of him. He's a famous climber."

She showed a spark of interest. "Really? Yes, now you mention it, he does sit every night poring over maps and things, or glued to the radio listening to this Everest climb they're making."

"That's who it is, then. He wrote a book once on Nanga Parbat."

"Oh?" said Marcia, losing interest. "Well, he goes round with another man, a queer little type called Hubert Hay. I don't think they came together, but I gather Hay's a writer as well. He's little and round and quite, quite sorbo."

"Sorbo?"

"Yes. Unsquashable."

"I see. But what an odd word. Sorbo . . . is it Italian?"

She gave a charming little choke of laughter. "My God, but that dates me, doesn't it? I'll have to watch myself. No, darling, it's not Italian. Some way back, in the thirties, when you were in your pram, they sold unsquashable rubber balls for children. Sorbo Bouncers, they were called."

"And you used to play with them?"

"Darling," said Marcia again. "But how sweet of you. . . . Anyway, the little man's definitely sorbo in nature *and* appearance, and wears fancy waistcoats. There's another man whose name I don't know, who got here last night. I've a feeling he writes, too."

"Good heavens."

"I know. Just a galaxy of talent, haven't we? Though probably none of them are any good. Sorbo is definitely not. But this chap looks as though he might be—all dark and damn-your-eyes," said Marcia poetically, then gloomed at her gin. "Only—he fishes, too."

"It sounds a very intriguing collection of people," I said.

"Doesn't it?" she said without conviction. "Oh, and there's an aged lady who I *think* is Cowdray-Simpson's mother and who knits *all the time,* my dear, in the most ghastly colors. And three youths with bare knees who camp near the river and come in for meals and go about with hammers and sickles and things—"

"Geology students, I'll bet," I said. "And I rather doubt the sickles. There's only one thing for it, you know. You'll have to take up fishing yourself. I'm going to. I'm told it's soothing for the nerves."

She shot me a look of horror mingled with respect. "My God! How marvellous of you! But—" Then her gaze fell on my left hand, and she nodded. "I might have known. You're married. I suppose he makes you. Now, if that wretched Mrs. Corrigan—"

"I'm not married," I said.

She caught herself. "Oh, sorry, I—"

"Divorced."

"O—oh!" She relaxed and sent me a vivid smile. "You too? My dear, so'm I."

"I know."

"*Three times,* honey. Too utterly exhausting, I may tell you. Aren't they stinkers?"

"I beg your pardon?"

"Men, darling. Stinkers."

"Oh, I see."

"Don't tell me yours wasn't a stinker too?"

"He was," I said. "Definitely."

"I knew it," said Marcia happily. I thought I had never seen two pink gins go further. "What was his name?"

"Nicholas."

"The beast," she said generously. The old crusading instinct was rising again, I could see. "Have another drink, Jeanette darling, and tell me *all* about it."

"This one's on me," I said firmly, and pressed the bell. "And my name is Gianetta. Gee-ann-etta. Of Italian origin, like sorbo."

"It's pretty," said she, diverted. "How come you've an Italian name?"

"Oh, it's old history. . . ." I ordered the drinks, glad to steer the conversation in a new direction. "My great-grandmother was called Gianetta. She's the kind of ancestress one wants to keep in the family cupboard, tightly locked away, only my great-grandmamma never let herself be locked away anywhere, for a moment."

"What did she do?" asked Marcia, intrigued.

"Oh, she took the usual road to ruin. Artists' model, artists' mistress, then married a baronet, and—"

"So did I once," said Marcia cheerfully. "I left him, though. Did she?"

"Of course. She bolted with a very advanced young artist to Paris, where she made a handsome fortune—don't ask me how—then died in a nunnery at the happy old age of eighty-seven."

"Those were the days." Marcia's voice was more than a little wistful. "Not the nunnery bit, but the rest. . . . What a thoroughly worthy great-grandmother to have— especially the bit about the fortune and the title."

I laughed. "They didn't survive. Mother was the only grandchild, and Gianetta left all her money to the convent —as fire insurance, I suppose." I put down my empty glass. "So—unlike my great-grandmamma—I wear clothes for a living."

Through the glass door I could see the Cowdray-Simpsons coming down the stairs. A maid bustled across the hall towards the dining room. Outside, behind the steep crest of Sgurr na Stri, the red of the sky was deepening to copper, its brightness throwing the jagged rock into towering relief. I saw three young men—the campers, no doubt—coming along from the river; they skirted the windows of the lounge, and a moment later I heard the porch door swing open and shut.

Somewhere, a clock struck seven.

"I'm hungry," I said. "Thank heaven it's dinnertime."

I got out of my chair, and moved to the window that faced east. Away in front of the hotel stretched the breadth of the valley floor, almost a mile of flat sheep-bitten turf, unbroken save by little peaty streams that here and there meandered seawards. The road, narrow and rutted, curved away across it, following the shore line, then lifted its grey length up through the heather and out of sight. To the right the sea murmured, pewter-dark now and unillumined in the shadow of the mountains. Far to the left, at Blaven's foot, a glimmer of water recalled the copper sky.

A late grouse shouted "Comeback!" and fell silent. A gull on the shore stretched its wings once, then settled them again upon its back. The sea seemed still. It was a prospect wild and dreary enough; no sound but a bird's call and a sheep's lament, no movement but the shake of a gull's wing and the stride of a latecomer walking un-hurriedly across the grass.

Then the walker trod on the gravel of the road. The scrunch of his boot on the rough surface startled the still-ness. A feeding snipe flashed up beside him, and fled up the glen in a zigzag of lightning flight. I saw the silver gleam of his underwings once, twice, against the tower-ing menace of Blaven, then I lost him.

"Blaven . . ." I said thoughtfully. "I wonder—"

Behind me, Marcia's voice was sharp and brittle. "Not any more of that, please. D'you mind?"

I looked back at her in surprise. She was gulping the last of her third gin, and across it she met my eyes queer-ly. Disconcerted, and a little shaken, as one always is by rudeness, I stared back at her. I had shifted the talk rather arbitrarily, I knew, to Gianetta and her misdeeds, but then I hadn't wanted to talk about Nicholas. And she had seemed interested enough. If I had been boring her—but she had not appeared to be bored. On the contrary.

She gave an apologetic little grin. "I can't help it," she said. "But don't let's. Please."

"As you wish," I said, a little stiffly. "I'm sorry." I turned back to the window.

The mountain met me, huge and menacing. And I looked at it in sudden enlightenment. *Blaven*. It had been my mention of Blaven, not of Gianetta, that had made Marcia retreat into her gin glass like a snail into its shell. Roderick Grant, and Murdo, and now Marcia Maling . . . or was I being over-imaginative? I stared out at the gathering dusk, where the latecomer was just covering the last twenty yards to the hotel door. Then my look narrowed on him. I stiffened, and looked again. . . .

"Oh my God," I said sharply, and went back into the room like a pea from a catapult.

I stopped on the hearthrug, just in front of a goggle-eyed Marcia Maling, and drew a long, long breath.

"Oh my *dear* God," I said again.

"What's up? Is it because I—?"

"It's not you at all," I said wearily. "It's the man who's just arriving at the front door of this hotel."

"Man?" She was bewildered.

"Yes. I presume he is your nameless, dark, damn-your-eyes writer . . . except that he doesn't happen to be name-less to me. His name is Nicholas Drury."

Her mouth opened. *"No! you mean—?"*

I nodded. "Just that. My husband."

"The—the stinker?"

I smiled mirthlessly. "Quite so. As you say. This holiday," I added without any conviction whatsoever, "is going to be *fun.*"

Chapter 3

YES, THERE IT WAS, as large as life, the arrogant black signature in the visitors' book: *Nicholas Drury, London. May 29th, 1953.* I looked down at it for a moment, biting my lip, then my eye was caught by another entry in the same hand, high up on the preceding page: *Nicholas Drury, London. April 28th, 1953.* He had been here already this summer, then. I frowned down at the book, wondering what on earth he could be doing in Skye. He must, of course, be collecting material for some book; he would hardly have chosen a place like this for a holiday. This Highland fastness, all trout and misty heather and men in shabby tweeds, accorded ill with what I remembered of Nicholas. I picked up the pen, conscious that my hands were not quite steady. All the carefully acquired poise in the world was not going to make it any more possible for me to meet Nicholas Drury again with the casual camaraderie which was, no doubt, fashionable among the divorcés of his London circle.

I dipped the pen in the inkstand, hesitated, and finally wrote: *Gianetta Brooke, Tench Abbas Rectory, Warwickshire.* Then I tugged my wedding ring rather painfully off my finger and dropped it into my bag. I would have to tell Major Persimmon, the hotel proprietor, why Mrs. Drury had suddenly become Miss Brooke: there were, it seemed to me, altogether too many embarrassments contingent on there being a Mr. and Mrs. Drury in the same hotel. Marcia Maling had already promised to say nothing. And Nicholas was not to know that I had not become Miss Brooke again four years ago. He would probably be as annoyed and uncomfortable as I, when we met, and would surely try to pass off the awkward encounter as easily as possible. So, at any rate, I assured myself, as I blotted and shut the book, though, remembering my handsome and incalculable husband as I did, I felt that there was very little dependence to be placed on the good behavior of Nicholas Drury.

Then I jumped like a nervous cat as a man's voice said behind me: "Janet Drury, as I live!"

I turned quickly, to see a man coming down the stairs towards me.

"Alastair! How nice to see you again! Where've you been all these years?"

Alastair Braine took both my hands and beamed down at me. He was a big, rugged-looking man, with powerful shoulders, perpetually untidy brown hair, and a disarming grin that hid an exceptionally shrewd mind. He looked anything but what he was—one of the coming men in the ruthless world of advertising.

"America mostly, with a dash of Brazil and Pakistan. You knew I was working for the Pergamon people?"

"Yes, I remember. Have you been back long?"

"About six weeks. They gave me a couple of months' leave, so I've come up here with some friends for a spot of fishing."

"It's lovely seeing you again," I said, "and I must say your tan does you credit, Alastair!"

He grinned down at me. "It's a pity I can't return the compliment, Janet, my pet. Not"—he caught himself up hastily—"that it's not lovely to see you, too, but you look a bit Londonish, if I may say so. What's happened to the schoolgirl complexion? Nick been beating you?"

I stared at him, but he appeared to notice nothing odd in my expression. He said, cheerfully: "He never told me you were joining us here, the scurvy devil."

"Oh Lord," I said. "Alastair, don't tell me you didn't know? We got a divorce."

He looked startled, even shocked. *Divorced?* When?"

"Over four years ago now. D'you mean to tell me you hadn't heard?"

He shook his head. "Not a word. Of course, I've been abroad all the time, and I'm the world's lousiest letter writer, and Nick's the next worst, so you can see—" He broke off and whistled a little phrase between his teeth. "Ah, well. Sorry, Janet. I—well, perhaps I'm not so very surprised, after all. . . . You don't mind my saying that?"

"Don't give it a thought." My voice was light and brittle, and would do credit, I thought, to any of Nicholas's casual London lovelies. "It was just one of those things that couldn't ever have worked. It was nobody's fault; he just thought I was another kind of person altogether. You see, in my job you tend to look—well, tough and sort of well-varnished, even when you're not."

"And you're not."

"Well, I wasn't then," I said. "I've a better veneer now."

"Three years of my great friend Nicholas," said Alastair, "would sophisticate a Vestal Virgin. Bad luck, Janet. But, if I may ask, what are you doing here?"

"Having a holiday like you, and dodging the Coronation crowds. I need hardly say I had no idea Nicholas was going to be here. I was a bit run down, and wanted somewhere restful, and I heard of the hotel through some friends of the family."

"Somewhere restful." He gave a little bark of laughter. "Oh my ears and whiskers! And you have to run slap into Nick!"

"Not yet," I told him grimly. "That's a pleasure in store for us both."

"Lord, Lord," said Alastair ruefully, then began to grin again. "Don't look so scared, my child. Nick won't eat you. It's he should be nervous, not you. Look, Janet, will you let me dine at your table tonight? I'm with a couple who could probably do with having to have a little of one another's society."

"I'd love you to," I said gratefully. "But how on earth is it that Nicholas didn't tell you about us?"

"I've really seen very little of him. He's apparently in Skye collecting stuff on folklore and suchlike for a book, and he's been moving from one place to another, with this as a main base. He's out most of the time. I did ask after you, of course, and he just said: 'She's fine. She's still with Hugo, you know. They've a show due soon.' I thought nothing of it."

"When was this?"

"Oh, when I first got here and found he was staying. May the tenth, or thereabouts."

"We *were* getting a show ready then, as it happens. But how on earth did he know?"

"Search me," said Alastair cheerily, and then turned

to greet the couple who were crossing the hall towards
us. The woman was slight, dark, and almost nondescript
save for a pair of really beautiful brown eyes, long-lidded
and flecked with gold. Her dress was indifferently cut, and
was a depressing shade of green. Her hair had no luster,
and her mouth drooped petulantly. The man with her was
a startling contrast. He, too, was dark, but his thinness
gave the impression of a great wiry strength and vitality.
His eyes were blue, dark Irish blue, and he was extraordi-
narily handsome, though there were lines round the sensi-
tive mouth that spoke of a temper too often given rein.

I said quickly: "The name's Brooke, Alastair, not
Drury. Do remember. I thought it might be awkward—"

"I couldn't agree more. Ah"—as they came up—"Hart,
Alma, this is Gianetta Brooke. Janet, Mr. and Mrs. Corrigan."

We murmured politely. I saw Mrs. Corrigan eyeing my
frock; her husband's blue eyes flicked over me once, with
a kind of casual interest, then they sought the lounge
door, as if he were waiting for someone else.

"I'm going to desert you at dinner, Alma, if you'll
forgive me." Alastair made his excuses. "Miss Brooke and
I are old friends, and we've a lot to talk about."

Mrs. Corrigan looked vaguely resentful, and I wondered for a moment if she were going to invite me to
join their table, until I realized that she was hesitating
between two evils, the hazard of having another woman
near her husband, and the loss of the society of her husband's friend. She had, in fact, the air of one for whom
life has for a long time been an affair of perpetual small
calculations such as this. I felt sorry for her. Through
Alastair's pleasant flow of conversational nothings, I shot
a glance at Hartley Corrigan, just in time to see the look
on his face as the lounge door opened behind me, and
Marcia Maling drifted towards us on a cloud of Chanel
No. 5. My pity for Alma Corrigan became, suddenly,
acute. She seemed to have no defenses. She simply stood
there, dowdy, dumb, and patently resentful, while Marcia,
including us all in her gay "How were the fish, my dears?"
enveloped the whole group in the warm exuberance of her
personality. The whole group, yes—but somehow, I
thought, as I watched her, and listened to some absurd
fish story she was parodying—somehow she had cut out

Hartley Corrigan from the herd, and penned him as neatly as if she were champion bitch at the sheep trials, and he were a marked wether. And as for the tall Irishman, it was plain that, for all he was conscious of the rest of us, the two of them might as well have been alone.

I found I did not want to meet Alma Corrigan's eyes, and looked away. I was wishing the gong would go. The hall was full of people now; all the members of Marcia's list seemed to be assembled. There were the Cowdray-Simpsons, being attentive to an ancient white-haired lady with a hearing aid; there, in a corner, were the two oddly assorted teachers, silent and a little glum; my friend of the boat, Roderick Grant, was consulting a barometer in earnest confabulation with a stocky individual who must be Ronald Beagle; and, deep in a newspaper, sat the unmistakable Hubert Hay, dapper and rotund in the yellowest of Regency waistcoats.

Then Nicholas came quickly round the corner of the stairs, and started down the last flight into the hall.

He saw me straightaway. He paused almost imperceptibly, then descended the last few stairs and came straight across the hall.

"Alastair," I said, under my breath, furious to find that my throat felt tight and dry.

Alastair turned, saw Nicholas, and took the plunge as smoothly as an Olympic swimmer.

"Hi, Nick!" he said. "Look who's here. . . . Do you remember Janet Brooke?"

He stressed the surname ever so slightly. Nicholas's black brows lifted a fraction of an inch, and something flickered behind his eyes. Then he said: "Of course. Hello, Gianetta. How are you?"

It came back to me sharply, irrelevantly, that Nicholas was the only person who had never shortened my name. I met his eyes with an effort, and said, calmly enough: "I'm fine, thank you. And you?"

"Oh, very fit. You're here on holiday, I take it?"

"Just a short break. Hugo sent me away. . . ." It was over, the awkward moment, the dreaded moment, sliding past in a ripple of commonplaces, the easy mechanical politenesses that are so much more than empty convention; they are the greaves and cuirasses that arm the naked nerve. And now we could turn from one another in relief, as we were gathered into the group of which Marcia Maling was still the radiant point. She had been talking to Hartley Corrigan, but I could see her watching Nicholas from under her lashes, and now she said, turning to me: "Another old friend, darling?"

I had forgotten for the moment that she was an actress, and stared at her in surprise, so beautifully artless had the question been. Then I saw the amusement at the back of her eyes, and said coolly: "Yes, another old friend. My London life is catching me up even here, it seems. Nicholas, let me introduce you to Miss Marcia Maling— *the* Marcia Maling, of course. Marcia, this is Nicholas Drury."

"*The* Nicholas Drury?" Marcia cooed it in her deepest, furriest voice, as she turned the charm full on to him with something of the effect that, we are told, a cosmic ray gun has when turned on to an earthly body. But Nicholas showed no sign of immediate disintegration. He merely looked ever so slightly wary as he murmured something conventional. He had seen that amused look of Marcia's, too, I knew. He had always been as quick as a cat. Then Hartley Corrigan came in with some remark to Marcia, and, in less time than it takes to write it, the whole party was talking about fish. The men were, at any rate; Marcia was watching Hartley Corrigan, Alma Corrigan watched Marcia, and I found myself studying Nicholas.

He had changed, in four years. He would be thirty-six now, I thought, and he looked older. His kind of dark, saturnine good looks did not alter much, but he was thinner, and, though he seemed fit enough, there was tension in the way he held his shoulders, and some sort of strain about his eyes, as if the skin over his cheekbones was drawn too tightly back into the scalp. I found myself wondering what was on his mind. It couldn't just be the strain of starting a new book, though some stages, I knew, were hell. No, knowing him as I did, I knew that it must be something else, some other obscure stress that I couldn't guess at, but which was unmistakably there. Well, at any rate, I thought, this time I couldn't possibly be the cause of his mood; and neither, this time, did I have to worry about it.

I was just busily congratulating myself that I didn't have to care any more, when the gong sounded, and we all went in to dinner.

Chapter 4

IT BECAME MORE THAN EVER OBVIOUS, after dinner, that the awkwardness of my own situation was by no means the only tension in the oddly assorted gathering at the Camasunary Hotel. I had not been overimaginative. That there were emotional undercurrents here seemed more than ever apparent, but I don't think I realized, at first, quite how strong they were. I certainly never imagined they might be dangerous.

By the time I got back into the lounge after dinner, the groups of people had broken and re-formed, and, as is the way in small country hotels, conversation had become general. I saw with a little twinge of wry amusement that Marcia Maling had deserted the Corrigans and was sitting beside Nicholas. It was, I supposed, a change for the better. She could no more help being pulled into the orbit of the nearest interesting man than she could help breathing, but I wished she would leave Hartley Corrigan alone. She had much better spend her time on Nicholas; he could look after himself.

Alastair found a chair for me in a corner, then excused himself and went off to see about weighing and dispatching the salmon he had caught that day. I saw Corrigan get up, without a word to his wife, and follow him from the room. Alma Corrigan sat without looking up, stirring and stirring her coffee.

"Will you have coffee? Black or white?"

I looked up to meet the bright gaze of the younger of the two teachers, who was standing in front of me with a cup in either hand. She had changed into a frock the color of dry sherry, with a cairngorm brooch in the lapel. It was a sophisticated color, and should not have suited her, but somehow it did; it was as if a charming child had dressed up in her elder sister's clothes. She looked younger than ever, and touchingly vulnerable.

I said: "Black, please. Thank you very much. But why should you wait on me?"

She handed me a cup. "Oh, nobody serves the coffee.

They bring it all in on a huge tray, and we each get our own. You've just come, haven't you?"

"Just before dinner." I indicated the chair at my elbow. "Won't you sit down? I've been deserted for a fish."

She hesitated, and I saw her shoot a glance across the room to where her companion was apparently deep in a glossy magazine. Then she sat down, but only on the edge of the chair, remaining poised, as it were, for instant flight.

"The fish certainly have it all their own way," she admitted. "I'm Roberta Symes, by the way."

"And I'm Gianetta Brooke. I take it you don't fish?"

"No. We're walking, Marion and I—that's Marion Bradford, over there. We're together. At least, we're climbing, sort of."

"What d'you mean by sort of?" I asked, amused. The Skye hills had not struck me as being the kind you could sort of climb.

"Well, Marion's a climber, and I'm not. That's really what I mean. So we go scrambling, which is a kind of halfway solution." She looked at me ingenuously. "But I'm *dying* to learn. I'd like to be as good as Mr. Beagle, and climb on every single Cuillin in turn, including the Inaccessible Pinnacle!"

"A thoroughly unworthy ambition," said a voice above us. Roderick Grant had come across, and was standing over us, coffee cup in hand.

Roberta's eyes widened. "Unworthy? That from *you*! Why, Mr. Grant?"

He turned and, with a sweep of one arm, indicated the prospect from the lounge windows.

"Look at them," he said. "Look at them. Thirty million years ago they thrust their way up from God knows where, to be blasted by wind and ice and storm, and chiseled into the mountain shapes you walk over today. They've been there countless ages, the same rocks, standing over the same ocean, worn by the same winds. And you, who've lived out a puny little twenty or thereabouts, talk of scaling them as if they were—"

"Teeth?" said Roberta, and giggled. "I know what you mean, though. They do make one feel a bit impermanent, don't they? But then it's all the more of a challenge, don't you feel? Mere man, or worse still mere woman, conquering the—the giants of time, climbing up—"

"Everest!" Colonel Cowdray-Simpson's exclamation

came so pat that I jumped, and Roberta giggled again. *The Times* rustled down an inch or two, and the Colonel peered over it at Nicholas, who was nearest the radio. "Turn on the wireless, will you, Drury? Let's hear how they're getting on."

Nicholas obeyed. The news was nearly over. We had luckily missed the conferences, the strikes, the newest atomic developments, the latest rumors from the U.S.S.R., and had come in just in time for a fuss about the seating in Westminster Abbey, a description of the arches in the Mall, and a hint of the general excitement in a London seething already towards its Coronation boiling point three days hence. And nothing yet, apparently, about Everest. . . .

Nicholas switched off.

"But I think they're going to make it," he said.

"It's too thrilling, isn't it?" said Marcia comfortably.

"It's certainly a magnificent effort," said Colonel Cowdray-Simpson. "They deserve their luck. What d'ye say, Beagle? What are the chances with the weather?"

"Fair enough." Beagle looked faintly uncomfortable at being thus appealed to in public. I remembered, with a quickening of interest, that this unassuming little man had been involved in an earlier attempt on Everest. But he seemed unwilling to pursue the subject. He groped in his jacket pocket and produced his pipe, turning the conversation abruptly. "I'd say they had a chance of better weather there than we have here, at any rate. I don't like the look of the sky. There's rain there."

"All the better for the fishing," said Mrs. Cowdray-Simpson placidly, but Roberta moaned.

"Oh *no*! And I wanted to start *really* climbing tomorrow."

"Quite determined to conquer the Cuillin, then?" said Roderick Grant.

"Quite!"

"Where d'you intend to start?"

"I don't know. I'm leaving that to Marion."

"Garsven's not hard," said someone—I think it was Alma Corrigan. "There's a way up from the Coruisk end—"

Marion Bradford interrupted: "The best first climbs are Bruach na Frithe and Sgurr na Banachdich, but they're too far away. Garsven is within reach, but of course it's just plain dull." Her flat voice and uncompromising manner fell hardly short, I considered, of being just plain rude. Alma Corrigan sat back in her chair with a little tightening of the lips. Roberta flushed slightly and leaned forward.

"Oh, but Marion, I'm sure Mrs. Corrigan's right. It doesn't look hard, and there must be a wonderful view——"

"There's a wonderful view from every single one of the Cuillins," said Marion dampingly.

"You've climbed them all?" asked Roderick gently.

"If you mean do I know what I'm talking about, the answer is yes," said Marion Bradford.

There was a little pause, in which everyone looked faintly uncomfortable, and I wondered what on earth made people behave like that without provocation. Colonel and Mrs. Cowdray-Simpson returned to *The Times* crossword, and Roderick Grant lit a cigarette, looking all at once impossibly remote and well-bred. Nicholas was looking bored, which meant, I knew, that he was irritated, and Marcia Maling winked across at me and then said something to him which made his mouth twitch. Roberta merely sat silent, fiery red and unhappy. As an exercise in Lifemanship, it had been superb.

Then Hubert Hay spoke for the first time, completely ignoring both Marion Bradford's rudeness and the hiatus in the conversation. I remembered Marcia's definition of him as sorbo, and felt amused.

"If I was you," he said cheerily to Roberta, "I'd try the Bad Step. Wait till high tide, and then you won't break your neck if you fall. You'll only drown. Much less uncomfortable, they say."

He had a curiously light, high little voice, and this, together with his odd appearance, produced a species of comic relief. Roberta laughed. "I can swim."

"In climbing boots and a rucksack?"

"Oh well, perhaps not!"

"What on earth's the Bad Step?" I asked.

Hubert Hay pointed towards the west windows. "You see that hill beyond the river's mouth, between us and the Cuillin?"

"Yes."

"That's Sgurr na Stri. It's a high tongue of land between here and the bay at the foot of Garsven. You can take a short cut across it, if you want a scramble. But if you follow the coast round to Loch Coruisk and the Cuillin, you have to cross the Bad Step."

"It sounds terrible. Is it a sort of Lovers' Leap?"

"Oh no. It's only a slab of gabbro tilted at a filthy angle —about sixty degrees—"

"Not as much," said Roderick Grant.

"No? Maybe you're right. Anyway, it hangs over the sea, and you have to cross it by a crack in the rock, where your nails can get a good grip."

"Your *nails*?" said Marcia, horror-stricken. "My God! D'you mean you have to *crawl* across?"

Nicholas grinned. "No, lady. He's talking about your boots."

"It sounds just my style," announced Roberta buoyantly. "After all, who minds drowning? Let's go around there, Marion, and come back over Sgurr na Stri."

"I've made up my mind where we're going," said Marion, in that flat, hard voice which carried so disastrously. "We're going up Blaven."

There was a sudden silence. I looked up sharply. I had been right, then, in thinking that some queer reaction took place every time that name was mentioned. This time it was unmistakable. And I was not imagining the note of defiance in Marion Bradford's voice. She knew that her announcement would fall on the room in just that kind of silence.

Ronald Beagle spoke then, diffidently. "Is that quite— er, wise, Miss Bradford? It's not exactly a beginner's scramble, is it?"

"It's easy enough up the ridge from this end," she said shortly.

"Oh, quite. But if the weather's bad—"

"A spot of rain won't hurt us. And if mist threatens we won't go. I've got that much sense."

He said no more, and silence held the room again for a moment. I saw Nicholas move, restlessly, and I wondered if he felt, as I did, a discomfort in the atmosphere sharper than even Marion Bradford's rudeness could warrant.

Apparently Marion herself sensed something of it, for she suddenly stabbed out her cigarette viciously into an ash tray and got up.

"In any case," she said, in that tight, aggressive voice of hers, "it's time *someone* broke the hoodoo on that blasted mountain, isn't it? Are you coming, Roberta?"

She stalked out of the room. Roberta gave me an un-comfortable little smile, and got up to follow her. For an instant I felt like advising her to stay, then decided that, whatever the crosscurrents of emotion that were wrecking the comfort of the party, I had better not add to them. I merely smiled at her, and she went out after her friend.

There was the inevitable awkward pause, in which everyone madly wanted to discuss Marion Bradford, but, naturally, couldn't. Then Marcia, who, as I was rapidly discovering, had no inhibitions at all, said:

"Well, really! I must say—"

Colonel Cowdray-Simpson cleared his throat rather hastily, and said, across her, to Ronald Beagle: "And where do you propose to go tomorrow, Beagle?"

"Weather permitting, sir, I'm going up Sgurr nan Gillean. But I'm afraid . . ."

I got to my feet. I had had enough of this, and I felt cramped and stale after my journey. And if Murdo and Beagle were right, and it was going to rain in the morning, I might as well go out now for an hour. As I turned to put my coffee cup on the tray, I saw, to my dismay, that Nicholas had risen too, and was coming across the room in my direction. It looked very much as if he was going to speak to me, or follow me out, and I felt, just then, that a tête-à-tête with Nicholas would be the final straw. I turned quickly towards the nearest woman, who happened to be Alma Corrigan.

"I'm going out for a short walk," I said, "and I don't know my way about yet at all. I wonder if you'd care to join me?"

She looked surprised, and, I thought, a little pleased. Then the old resentful look shut down on her face again, and she shook her head.

"I'd have liked to very much." She was politely final. "But, if you'll forgive me, I'm a bit tired. We've been out all day, you know."

Since she had already told me, before dinner, that she had spent the day sitting on a boulder while the men fished the Strath na Creitheach, this was a very efficient rebuff.

"Of course," I said, feeling a fool. "Some other time, perhaps." I turned away to find Roderick Grant at my elbow.

"If I might—?" He was looking diffidently down at me. "There's a very pleasant walk up to the loch, if you'll let me be your guide. But perhaps you prefer to go alone?"

"By no means," I assured him. Nicholas had stopped when Roderick Grant spoke, and I knew that he was frowning. I smiled back at Mr. Grant. "Thanks very much. I'll be glad of your company."

Nicholas had not moved. I had to pass him on my way to the door. For a second our glances met. His eyes, hard and expressionless, held mine for a full three seconds, then he gave a twisted little smile and deliberately turned back to Marcia Maling.

I went to get my coat.

Chapter 5

AT HALF PAST NINE on a summer's evening in the Hebrides, the twilight has scarcely begun. There is, perhaps, with the slackening of the day's brilliance, a somber note overlying the clear colors of sand and grass and rock, but this is no more than the drawing of the first thin blue veil. Indeed, night itself is nothing but a faint dusting-over of the day, a wash of silver through the still-warm gold of the afternoon.

The evening was very still, and, though the rain-threatening clouds were slowly packing higher behind us in the southwest, the rest of the sky was clear and luminous. Above the ridge of Sgurr na Stri, above and beyond the jagged peaks of the Cuillin, the sun's warmth still lingered in the flushed air. Across this swimming lake of brightness one long bar of cloud lay sullenly, one thin line of purple shadow, struck from below to molten brilliance by the rays of a now invisible sun.

We turned northwards up the valley, and our steps on the short sheep turf made no sound in the stillness. The flat pasture of the estuary stretched up the glen for perhaps half a mile, then the ground rose, steep and broken, to make the lower spurs and hillocks that were Blaven's foothills. One of these, the biggest, lay straight ahead of us, a tough little heather-clad hill which blocked the center of the glen and held the southern shore of the loch. To the left of it curved the river; on the east a ridge of rock and heather joined it to the skirts of Blaven.

"Isn't there a path along the river?" I asked.

"Oh, yes, but if you want to climb An't Sròn—that hill in front—for a view of the loch, we'd better keep to the Blaven side of the glen. There's a bog farther on, near the river, which isn't too pleasant."

"Dangerous, you mean, or merely wet?"

"Both. I don't know whether it would actually open and swallow you up, but the ground shakes in a beastly fashion, and you start to sink if you stand still. The deer avoid it."

"Then," I said with a shiver, "by all means let us avoid it too. It seems I ought to be very grateful to you for coming with me!"

He laughed. "It's actually pure selfishness on my part. If one loves a place very much one likes to show it off. I wasn't going to miss a fresh opportunity for taking credit to myself for this scenery. It must be one of the loveliest corners of the world."

"This particular corner, do you mean, or Skye and the Islands in general?"

"This bit of Skye." His hands were thrust deep into his pockets, but his eyes lifted briefly to the distant peaks, and to the great blue heights of Blaven dwarfing the glen where we walked. "Those."

"Is this your home, Mr. Grant?"

He shook his head. "No I was born among mountains, but very different ones. My father was minister of a tiny parish away up in the Cairngorms, a little lost village at the back of the north wind. Auchlechtie, at the foot of Bheinn a' Bhùird. D'you know it?"

"I'm afraid not."

He grinned. "I've never yet met anyone who did. . . . Well, that's where I learned my mountain worship! I'd no mother; my father was a remote kind of man, who had very little time for me; it was miles to school, so as often as not I just ran wild in the hills."

"You must have been a very lonely little boy."

"Perhaps I was. I don't remember. I don't think I felt lonely." He grinned again. "That is, until an uncle died, and left us a lot of money, and my father made me put shoes on and go to a public school to learn manners."

"That was bad luck."

"I hated it, of course. Particularly the shoes."

"And now you spend your time climbing?"

"Pretty well. I travel a bit—but I always seem to end up here, at any rate in May and June. They're the best months in the West, although"—he flung a quick glance over his shoulder—"I think our friend Beagle was right about the weather. We'll have rain tomorrow, for certain, and once the Cuillin get a good grip on a rainstorm, they're very reluctant to let it go."

"Oh dear," I said, "and I was wanting to walk. I begin to see why people take up fishing here. It must be sheer self-defense."

"Very possibly. Watch your step, now. It's tricky going in this light."

We had reached the foot of the little hill called An't Sròn, and began to climb the rough heathery slope. A cock grouse rose with a clap from somewhere near at hand, and planed down towards the river, chakking indignantly. The light had faded perceptibly. Like an enormous storm cloud above the valley Blaven loomed, and behind his massive edge hung, now, the ghost of a white moon past the full.

Roderick Grant paused for a moment in his stride, and looked thoughtfully up at the wicked ridges shouldering the sky.

"I wonder if those two fool women will really go up there tomorrow?"

"Is it a bad climb?"

"Not if you know which way to go. Straight up the south ridge it's only a scramble. But there are nasty places even there."

"Miss Bradford said she knew her way about," I said.

A smile touched his mouth. "She did, didn't she? Well, we can't do much about it."

"I suppose not." We were more than halfway up the little hill. The going was getting steeper and rougher. "Mr. Grant," I said, a little breathlessly.

"Yes?"

I hesitated, then said flatly: "What did Miss Bradford mean about a hoodoo on Blaven? What's wrong with it?"

He stopped and glanced down at me. He looked surprised, almost blank. "Wrong with it?" He repeated the phrase half mechanically.

"Yes. Why does everyone shy off it like that? I'm sure they do. I can't be mistaken. And if it comes to that, what's wrong with the people in the hotel? Because there's *something*, and if you haven't noticed it—"

"*You don't know?*"

"Of course I don't know!" I said, almost irritably. "I've only just arrived. But even to me the setup seems uncomfortably like the opening of a bad problem play."

"You're not far astray at that," said Roderick Grant. "Only we're halfway through the play, and it looks as if the problem isn't going to be solved at all." He paused, and looked gravely down at me in the gathering dusk. "It's a nasty problem, too," he said. "The nastiest of all, in fact. There's been murder done."

I took a jerky little breath. *"Murder?"*

He nodded. His blue eyes, in that light, were dark under lowered brows. "Two and a half weeks ago it happened, on the thirteenth of May. It was a local girl, and she was murdered on Blaven."

"I—see." Half unbelievingly I lifted my eyes to the great mass ahead. Then I shivered and moved forward. "Let's get to the top of this hill," I said, "and then, if you don't mind, I think you'd better tell me about it."

We sat on a slab of rock, and lit cigarettes. Away below us, cradled in its purple hollow, Loch na Creitheach gleamed with a hard bright light like polished silver. Two ducks flew across it, not a foot above their own reflections.

"Who was the girl?" I asked. "And who did it?"

He answered the latter question first. "We still don't know who did it. That's what I meant when I said it was a nasty problem. The police—" He frowned down at the cigarette in his fingers, then said: "I'd better start at the beginning, hadn't I?"

"Please do."

"The girl's name was Heather Macrae. Her father's a crofter, who does some ghillying for the hotel folks in summertime. You'll probably meet him. His croft's three or four miles up the Strath na Creitheach, the river that flows into the far end of this loch. . . . Well, it seems Heather Macrae was 'keeping company' with a lad from the village, one Jamesy Farlane, and so, when she took to staying out a bit later in the long spring evenings, her folk didn't worry about it. They thought they knew who she was with."

"And it wasn't Jamesy after all?"

"Jamesy says not. He says it very loud and clear. But then, of course," said Roderick Grant, "he would."

"And if it wasn't Jamesy, who could it have been?"

"Jamesy says he and Heather had a quarrel—yes, he admits it quite openly. He says she'd begun to avoid him, and when finally he tackled her with it, she flared up and said she was going with a better chap than he was. A gentleman, Jamesy says she told him." He glanced at me. "A gentleman from the hotel."

"Oh *no*!" I said.

"I'm afraid so."

"But—that doesn't mean the man from the hotel was necessarily—"

"The murderer? I suppose not, but there's a strong probability—if, that is, he existed at all. We only have Jamesy Farlane's word for that. What we do know is that Heather Macrae went out on the evening of May the thirteenth to meet a man. She told her parents that she 'had a date.' "

"And—on Blaven, you said?"

His voice was somber. "This bit isn't nice, but I'd better tell you. At about midnight that night, some men who were out late on Loch Scavaig—I suspect they were poaching sea trout—saw what looked like a great blaze of fire halfway up Blaven. They were mystified, but of course not alarmed. It's bare rock, so they weren't afraid of its spreading. They went on with their job, whatever it was, and kept an eye on the fire. One of them had a look through some night glasses, and said it was a column of flame, like a big bonfire, but that its base was out of sight behind a rocky bluff."

He paused. "Well, they got more and more puzzled. Who on earth would light a bonfire away up there, and what on earth could he be burning there anyway? Whether they were being wise after the event, or not, I don't know, but one of them, Rhodri MacDowell, says that gradually, watching that leaping column of fire where no fire ought to be, they grew first of all uneasy, then alarmed, then downright frightened. And when the chap with the glasses reported seeing a dark figure moving in front of the flames, they decided to investigate."

He frowned down at the shining loch. "By the time they got to it, of course, the fire was out, and it was only the remains of the smoke licking up the rock face that guided

them. They found a widish ledge—easy enough to get to
—with the remains of charred driftwood and birch and
heather blackened and scattered, deliberately it seemed,
all over the rock. Lying in the middle of the blackened
patch was Heather's body, flat on its back." He drew
sharply on his cigarette, and his voice was flat and color-
less. "She was not very much burned. She had been dead
when he put her there. Ashes had been scattered over her,
and her throat was cut."

"Oh, dear God," I said.

"She was," said Roderick, in that flat, impersonal voice,
"fully clothed, and she was lying quietly, with her hands
crossed on her breast. The oddest thing was, though, that
she was barefooted, and all her jewelry had been taken
off."

"Jewelry?" I said, astounded. "But good heavens—"

"Oh no, not stolen," he said quickly. "She hadn't anything worth stealing, poor child, let alone worth getting
herself murdered for. It was all there, in a little pile in the
corner of the ledge: her shoes, a leather belt, and all
the ornaments she'd been wearing—a ring, a cheap bracelet and brooch, earrings—even a couple of hair clips. Odd,
don't you think?"

But I wasn't thinking about its oddness. I said savagely:
"The poor kid had certainly put on all her finery for him,
hadn't she?"

He shot me a look. "It's quite particularly unpleasant,
isn't it?"

"It certainly is." I looked up and along the towering
curve of Blaven's south ridge. "And the police: do they
favor Jamesy, or the gentleman from the hotel?"

He shrugged, and ground his cigarette out on the rock.
"God knows. They've been coming and going ever since
that day, putting us all through it—very quietly and unob-
trusively, but nevertheless thoroughly. But you see why
nerves are a little bit on edge?"

"I see," I said grimly. "I must say it seems a little
strange that Major Persimmon didn't warn new guests of
what was going on. They might even have preferred not
to come."

"Quite," said Roderick Grant. "But his line is, obviously, that Jamesy's talking nonsense to protect himself,
and that it's nothing to do with the hotel. The heavy questioning is all over, and the police are in any case being

very quiet about it all. You can hardly expect Bill—Major Persimmon—to ruin his season, and possibly his hotel, can you?"

"I suppose not." I squashed out my cigarette, and rose. He got up too, and stood looking down at me.

"I hope this hasn't upset you too much," he said, a little awkwardly.

"If it has," I said, "it can hardly matter, can it? It's that poor child, going up to her death on the mountain, all decked out in her best. . . ." I bit my lip, and kicked at a tuft of heather, then raised my head and looked straight at him. "Just tell me," I said, "precisely which 'gentlemen' were in this hotel on May the thirteenth?"

The blue eyes met mine levelly. "All those," he said expressionlessly, "who are here now, with the exception of Miss Maling's chauffeur."

"And which of you," I said doggedly, feeling unhappy and absurd at the same time, "has an alibi?"

"None of us that I know of." Nothing in his voice betrayed any awareness of the change of pronoun which all at once gave the story a horrible immediacy. "Two of those boys camping by the river swear they were together; the third, no. Colonel Cowdray-Simpson and Bill Persimmon are vouched for by their wives, but that counts for very little, of course. Corrigan and Braine were out fishing on Loch an Athain."

"At *midnight*?"

"Quite a lot of people do. It's never really dark at this time of the year."

"Then they were together?"

"No. They separated to different beats some time after eleven, and went back to the hotel in their own time. Mrs. Corrigan says her husband got in well before midnight."

There was an odd note in his voice, and I took him up sharply. "You don't believe her?"

"I didn't say that. I only think it was pretty good going to get back to Camasunary by midnight. Loch an Athain's another mile beyond the end of Creitheach, and the going's heavy."

"Did he let himself into the hotel?"

"It's open all night."

"How nice," I said. "And Mr. Hay?"

"In bed. A very difficult alibi to break."

"Or prove."

"As you say. Mine happens to be the same."

"I—I'm sorry," I said, feeling suddenly helpless. "This is—fantastic, isn't it? I can't *believe* . . . and anyway, I've no earthly business to be questioning you as if you were Suspect Number One. I really am sorry."

He grinned. "That's all right. And it is your business, after all, if you're going to stay here. You've got to judge whom, if anyone, you feel safe with."

I put a hand to my cheek. "Oh Lord," I said, "I suppost so. I—I hadn't thought of that."

He spoke quickly, with contrition. "And I'm a fool to have mentioned it before we got back to lights and company. . . . Come along." He took my arm and turned quickly, helping me over the boulder-strewn turf. "We'll get back to the hotel. After all, for all you know, I *might* be Suspect Number One. This way; there's a path along the top of the ridge. We'll follow it along the hill a bit before we go down."

I went with him, disconcerted to find that my heart was pumping violently. The night had grown perceptibly darker. We had our backs to the lucent west, and before us the ghost moon swam in a deepening sky, where the mass of Blaven stooped like Faustus's mountain, ready to fall on us.

And its menacing shape was repeated, oddly, in a shadow that loomed in front of us, right in our path . . . a tall pile of something, heaped on the heather as if to mark the crest of the hill. Roderick Grant guided me past it without a look, but I glanced back at it uncertainly.

"What's that? A cairn?"

He flicked a casual look over his shoulder. "That? No. It's a bonfire."

I stopped dead, and his hand fell from my arm. He turned in surprise. I noticed all at once how still the glen was, how still and lonely. The lights of the hotel seemed a very long way off.

I said: "A—a bonfire?" and my voice came out in a sort of croak.

He was staring at me. "Yes. What's up?" Then his voice changed. "Oh my God, I've done it again, haven't I? I never thought—I didn't mean to scare you. I'm a fool. . . ." He took two strides back towards me, and his hands were on my shoulders. "Miss—Janet"—I doubt if either of us really noticed his use of my name—"don't be frightened. It's only the local Coronation celebration. They've been collecting stuff for the bonfire for weeks! It's nothing more sinister than that!" He shook me gently. "And I promise you I'm not a murderer either!"

"I never thought you were," I said shakily. "It's I who'm the fool. I'm sorry."

His hands dropped to his sides, and I saw him smiling down in the dusk. "Then let's get back to the hotel, shall we?" he said.

We turned towards the lights of Camasunary.

After all, it was not so very late. The hotel was bright and warm and safe, and one or two people were still about. Through the lounge door I could see Hartley Corrigan and Alastair sitting over a last drink, and, nearby, Ronald Beagle placidly reading.

And the idea that any of the men that I had met could be guilty of a crime at once so revolting and so bizarre was fantastic enough to border on lunacy. It was on a slightly shamefaced note that I said good night to Roderick Grant, and went up to my room.

The head of the staircase opened on the central point of the main upper corridor, which was like a large E, its three branches all ending in windows facing east, over the front of the hotel. My room lay in the far southeastern corner, at the end of the lower arm of the E. The bathroom next to me was, I found, occupied, so, wrapping my white velvet housecoat round me, I set out in search of another, which I found eventually at the far end of the main corridor. I took a long time over my bath, and by the time I had finished the hotel seemed to have settled into silence for the night. I let myself quietly out of the bathroom, and padded back along the now darkened corridor.

I went softly across the head of the stairs, and was almost past before I realized that someone was standing, still and quiet, at the end of the passage opposite, silhouetted against the dim window. Almost with a start, I glanced over my shoulder.

It was two people. They had not seen me, and for a very good reason. They were in one another's arms, kissing passionately.

The woman was Marcia Maling. I recognized the fall of her pale hair even before her scent reached my nostrils. I remember vaguely thinking "Fergus?"—and then I recognized, too, the set of the man's shoulders, and the shape of his head.

Not Fergus. Nicholas.

Hurriedly I looked away, and went softly down the main corridor towards my room.

Somewhere behind me, on the other side of the passage, I heard a door shut softly.

Chapter 6

IT WAS PRECISELY ONE FORTY-EIGHT A. M. when I decided that I was not going to be able to sleep, and sat up in bed, groping for the light switch. The tiny illuminated face of my traveling clock stared uncompromisingly back at me from the bedside table. One forty-eight A. M. I scowled at it, and pressed the switch. Nothing happened. Then I remembered that the hotel made its own electricity, and that this was turned off at midnight. There had been a candlestick, I recollected . . . my hand groped and found it. I struck a match and lit the candle.

I scowled at the clock again, then slipped out of bed. I was jaded and depressed, and I knew that I had already reached the stage when my failure to sleep was so actively irritating that sleep had become an impossibility. What was worse, I knew I was in for one of the blinding nervous headaches that had devastated me all too often in the last three or four years. I could feel the warning now, like electric wire thrilling behind my eyes, pain, with the elusive threat of worse pain to come.

I sat on the edge of the bed, pressing my hands hard against my eyes, trying to will the pain away, while still in my wincing brain whirled and jostled the images that, conspiring to keep sleep at bay, had switched the agonizing current along my nerves. . . . Fire at midnight . . . fire on Blaven . . . and *a gentleman from the hotel.* Corrigan? Roderick? Alastair? Nicholas?

I shivered, then flinched and stood up. I wasn't even going to try to ride this one out; I was going to dope myself out of it, and quickly. The life-saving tablets were in my handbag. I padded across the room to get it, groping vaguely among the grotesque shadows that distorted the corners of the room. But it wasn't on the dressing table. It wasn't on the mantlepiece. Or on the floor near the hand basin. Or by the bed. Or—it was by now a search of despair—under the bed. It wasn't anywhere in the room.

I sat down on the bed again, and made myself acknowledge the truth. I hadn't taken my handbag on that walk with Roderick Grant. I had left it in the lounge. I could see it in my mind's eye, standing there on the floor beside my chair, holding that precious pillbox, as remote from me as if it had been on a raft in the middle of the Red Sea. Because nothing, I told myself firmly, wincing from a fresh jag of pain, *nothing* was going to get me out of my room that night. If anyone was to perform the classic folly of taking a midnight stroll among the murderous gentlemen with whom the hotel was probably packed, it was not going to be me.

On this eminently sensible note I got back into bed, blew out the candle, and settled down to ride it out.

Seventeen minutes later I sat up, lit the candle again, got out of bed, and grabbed my housecoat. I had reached, in seventeen minutes of erratically increasing pain, an even more sensible decision—and how much this was a product of reason and how much of desperation I can now judge more accurately than I could then. It was quite a simple decision, and very satisfactory. I had decided that Jamesy Farlane had murdered Heather Macrae. And since Jamesy Farlane didn't live in the hotel, I could go and get my tablets in perfect safety.

Perfect safety, I told myself firmly, thrusting my feet into my slippers and knotting the girdle of my housecoat tightly round me—as long as I was *very* quick, and *very* quiet, and was prepared to scream like blazes if I saw or heard the least little thing . . . .

Without pausing to examine the logic of this corollary to my decision, I seized my candle, unlocked my door, and set off.

And at once I saw that this was not to be, after all, the classic walk through the murder-haunted house, for, although the corridor lights were of course unlit, the glimmer from the eastern windows was quite sufficient to show me my way, and to lay bare the quiet and reassuring emptiness of the passages, flanked by their closed doors. I went softly along the main corridor, shielding my candle, until I reached the stairhead.

The staircase sank down into shadows, and I hesitated for a moment, glancing involuntarily over my shoulder towards the window where I had seen Marcia and Nicholas. No one was there, this time; the window showed an empty oblong framing the pale night. I could see, quite distinct against the nebulous near-light of the sky, the massive outline of Blaven's shoulder. The moon had gone.

Then I heard the whispering. I must have been listening to it, half unconsciously, during the few seconds I had been standing there, for when at length my conscious mind registered, with a jerk, the fact that two people were whispering behind the door to my right, I knew immediately that the sound had been going on all along.

It should have reassured me to know that someone else was still awake; it certainly shouldn't have disturbed and frightened me, but that is just what it did. There was, of course, no reason why someone else in the hotel should not be sleepless too. If Colonel Cowdray-Simpson and his wife, or the Corrigans, were wakeful, and consequently talkative, at this ungodly hour, they would certainly keep their voices down to avoid disturbing the other guests. But there was something about the quality of the whispering that was oddly disquieting. It was as if the soft, almost breathless ripple of sound in the darkness held some sort of desperation, some human urgency, whether of anger or passion or fear, which communicated itself to me through the closed panels, and made the hairs prickle along my forearms as if a draught of chilly wind had crept through a crack in the door.

I turned to go, and a board creaked as my weight shifted.

The whispering stopped. It stopped as abruptly as an engine shuts off steam. Silence dropped like a blanket, so that in a matter of seconds the memory of the sound seemed illusory, while the silence itself surged with millions of whisperings, all equally unreal. But the sense of desperation was still there, even in the silence. It was as if the stillness were a held breath, that might burst at any moment in a scream.

I moved quickly away—and tripped over a pair of shoes which had been standing in the corridor waiting to be cleaned in the morning. The carpet was thick, but the small sound, in that hush, was like thunder. I heard a muffled exclamation from behind the door, then, staccato, sibilant, the splutter of a question. A deeper voice said something in reply.

There was only one pair of shoes: a woman's. I hastily retrieved the one I had kicked over, and put it back beside its fellow. They were handmade Laforgues, exquisite, absurd things with four-inch heels. Marcia Maling's.

There was silence now behind the door. I almost ran down the stairs, plunging, heedless of the streaming candle flame, into the darker depths of the hall. I felt angry and ashamed and sick, as if I myself had been caught out in some questionable action. God knew, I thought bitterly, as I crossed the hall and pushed open the glass door of the lounge, it was none of my business, but all the same. . . . She had, after all, only met Nicholas tonight. And where was Fergus in all this? Surely I hadn't misread the hints she had dropped about Fergus? And where, too, did Hartley Corrigan come in, I wondered, remembering the look in his eyes, and, even more significantly, the look on his wife's face.

And here I paid for my speed and my heedlessness as the swing door rushed shut behind me and tore the flame from my candle into a long streamer of sharp-smelling smoke. Shadows surged up towards me, pouncing from the corners of the dim lounge, and I halted in my tracks and put a hand back to the door, already half in retreat towards the safety of my room. But the lounge was untenanted save by those shadows; in the glow of the banked peat fire I could see it all now clearly enough. I threw one haunted glance back at the hall beyond the glass door, then I went very quietly across the lounge towards where I knew my handbag ought to lie.

Marcia and Nicholas . . . the coupled names thrust themselves back into my mind. The odd thing about it, I thought, was that one couldn't dislike Marcia Maling—though I might feel differently about it if, like Mrs. Corrigan, I had a man to lose. It was to be supposed—I skirted a coffee table with some care—it was to be supposed that she couldn't help it. There was a long and ugly name for her kind of woman, but, remembering her vivid, generous beauty as she sat opposite me in this very room, I could not find it in me to dislike her. She was impossible, she was wanton, but she was amusing, and very lovely, and, I thought, kind. Perhaps she was even being kind to me,

in a queer way, by attracting Nicholas's attention to herself
when she guessed I wished to escape it—though this, I
felt, was perhaps giving a little too much credit to Miss
Maling's disinterested crusading spirit.

I grinned wryly to myself as I stooped and groped beside
the chair for my precious handbag. My fingers met nothing.
I felt anxiously along the empty floor, sweeping my hands
round in little questing circles that grew wider and more
urgent with failure . . . and then I saw the faint glint of
the bag's metal clasp, not on the floor, but on a level with
my eye as I stooped. Someone must have picked it up and
put it on the bookshelf beside the chair. I grabbed it,
yanked out with it some magazines and a couple of books,
and flew back across the lounge with my skirts billowing
behind me.

I was actually at the glass door, and shoving it open with
my shoulder, when I heard the outer door of the hotel
porch open, very quietly. I stood stock-still, clutching
books and bag and dead candle to a suddenly thudding
heart.

Someone came softly into the porch. I heard the scrape
of a nailed boot on the flags, and faint sounds as he moved
about among the climbing and fishing gear that always
cluttered the place. I waited. Roderick Grant had told me
the hotel stayed open all night. This was surely—*surely*—
nothing more sinister than some late fisherman, putting
his things away. That was all.

But all the same, I was not going to cross the hall and
climb the stairs in full view of him, whoever he was. So I
waited, trying to still my sickening heartbeats, backing
away from the glass door as I remembered my white
housecoat.

Then the outer door opened and shut again, just as softly as before, and, clear in the still night, I heard his boots
crunch once, twice, on the gravel road. I hesitated only for
a moment, then I shouldered aside the glass door and flew
across the hall to the outer porch, peering after him
through the window.

The valley was mist-dimmed, and full of vague shadows,
but I saw him. He had stepped off the gravel onto the
grass and was walking quickly away, head bent, along the
verge of the road towards Strathaird. A man, slim, tallish,
who walked with a long swinging stride. I saw him pause

once, and turn, looking back over his shoulder, but his face was no more than a dim blur. Then he vanished into the shadows.

I turned back from the window in the not-quite-darkness, gazing round the little porch. My eyes had adjusted themselves now. I could see the table, with its weighing machine and the white enamel trays for fish; the wicker chairs holding rucksacks, boots, fishing nets; pale ovals of climbing rope depending from pegs; coats and mackintoshes, scarves and caps, fishing rods and walking sticks. . . .

Behind me the door opened without a sound, and a man came quietly in out of the night.

I didn't scream, after all. Perhaps I couldn't. I merely dropped everything with a crash that seemed to shake the hotel, then stood, dumb and paralyzed, with my mouth open.

The porch door swung to with a bang behind him. He jerked out a startled oath, and then, with a click, a torch beam shot out and raked me, blindingly.

He said: "Janet!" And then laughed. "My God, but you startled me! What on earth are you doing down here at this hour?"

I blinked into the light, which went off.

"Alastair?"

"The same." He swung his haversack from his shoulder, and began to take off his Burberry. "What was that you dropped? It sounded like an atom bomb."

"Books, mostly," I said. "I couldn't sleep."

"Oh." He laughed again, and pitched his coat over a chair. "You looked like a ghost standing there in that white thing. I was unmanned, but positively. I nearly screamed."

"So did I." I stooped to pick up my things. "I'd better go back to bed."

He had a foot up on one of the chairs. "If you'd stay half a minute more and hold the torch for me, Janet, I could get these blasted bootlaces undone. They're wet."

I took the torch. "Is it raining?"

"In fits and starts."

"You've been fishing, I suppose?"

"Yes. Up the Strath."

"Any luck?"

"Pretty fair. I got two or three good fish, and Hart took a beauty. One and a half pounds."

"Hart? Oh—Hartley Corrigan."

"Mm. Don't wave the light about, my girl."

"Sorry. Is Mr. Corrigan not back yet, then?"

"Lord, yes. He came back a couple of hours since, but I'd just had some good rises, so I stayed. Strictly illegal, of course, so don't tell on me, will you?"

"Illegal?"

"It's the Sabbath, my dear. Had you forgotten? I should have stopped at midnight, like Hart." He pulled his second boot off, and straightened up.

"His fish aren't in the tray," I said.

"What?" His eyes followed the torch beam to the table. "Neither are they . . . that's odd."

"Alastair."

He turned his head sharply at the note in my voice.

"Well?"

I said, baldly: "Someone came into this porch five minutes ago, messed around for a bit, and then went out again."

"What? Oh—" he laughed. "Don't sound so worried! That would be Jamesy."

"Jamesy?"

"Jamesy Farlane; he was out with us. He's a better walker than I am, and he was in a hurry. He lives some way over towards Strathaird."

"I see," I said. I swallowed hard.

"Did you think he was a burglar? You don't need to worry about such urban horrors here, Janet. Nobody locks their doors in the Islands. There aren't such things as thieves."

"No," I said. I put the torch down on the table, and turned to go. "Only murderers."

I heard the sharp intake of his breath.

"Who told you?"

"Roderick Grant."

"I see. Worried?"

"Naturally."

He said: "I shouldn't be. Whatever it is all about, it can't touch you."

"I wasn't worried about myself."

"Who, then?" He sounded wary.

I said, with an edge to my voice: "Heather Macrae, of

course. The girl—and her people. What had she done that a filthy grotesque thing like that should catch up with her? What was it all about? There's something more than queer about it, Alastair. I can't explain just how I feel about it, but it—it's somehow particularly nasty."

He said, inadequately: "Murder's never pretty."

"But it can be plain," I said, "and this isn't just plain wicked murder. She wasn't just hit or stabbed or choked in a fit of human passion. She was deliberately done to death, and then—arranged. It was cold-blooded, calculating, and—and *evil*. Yes, evil. Here, too, of all places, where you'd think that sort of perverted ugliness had no existence. It's haunting me, Alastair."

He said, a little lamely: "The police are still on it, and they won't let up, you know."

I said: "Who do you think did it?"

"Janet—"

"You must have thought about it. Who? Jamesy Farlane?"

"I—look, Janet, I wouldn't talk too much about it—"

I said: "You mean, in case it's someone in the hotel?"

He said uncomfortably: "Well—"

"*Do* you think it's someone in the hotel?"

"I don't know. I—don't—know. If it frightens you, my dear, why don't you go somewhere else? Broadford, or Portree, or—"

"I'm staying here," I said. "I want to be here when they do nose out this devil, whoever he is. *Whoever* he is."

He was silent.

I said: "Good night, Alastair," and went back upstairs to my room.

I never took the tablets, after all. My dead-of-night walk among the murderers must have been the kind of shock therapy that my headache needed, for when I got back to my room I realized that the pain had completely gone.

I got into bed and surveyed the rest of my booty.

I had got, I discovered, two copies of *The Autocar*. The books were *The Bride of Lammermoor*, and the abridged edition of Frazer's *Golden Bough*.

The Bride of Lammermoor put me to sleep in something under ten minutes.

Chapter 7

NEXT MORNING, SURE ENOUGH, IT WAS RAINING, with a small, persistent, wetting rain. The sheep grazing in the glen near the hotel looked damp and miserable, and all but the nearest landmarks were invisible. Even Sgurr na Stri, just beyond the river, was dim in its shroud of grey.

When I came down, a little late, to breakfast, the place was quiet, though this was the Sabbath quiet rather than a depression due to the weather. I could see Alastair Braine and the Corrigans sitting over newspapers in the lounge, while Mrs. Cowdray-Simpson and the old lady had already brought their knitting into play. There were, however, signs that even a wet Sunday in the Highlands could not damp some enthusiasms: Colonel Cowdray-Simpson, at the grille of the manager's office, was conducting a solemn discussion on flies with Mr. Persimmon and a big country-man in respectable black; Marion Bradford and Roberta were in the porch, staring out at the wet landscape; and near them Roderick Grant bent, absorbed, over a landing net that he was mending with a piece of string.

He looked up, saw me, and grinned. "Hullo. It's too bad it's Sunday, isn't it? Wouldn't you have loved a nice day's fishing in the rain?"

"No, thank you," I said with decision. "I suppose this is what you fishing maniacs call ideal weather?"

"Oh, excellent." He cocked an eye at the sullen prospect. "Though it mightn't prove too dismal even for lay-men. This is the sort of day that can clear up in a flash. Miss Symes might get her climb after all."

"Do you think so?" Roberta turned eagerly.

"It's possible. But"—he shot a wary half glance at Marion Bradford's back, still uncompromisingly turned—"be careful if you do go, and don't get up too high. The mist can drop again as quickly as it can rise."

He had spoken quietly, but Marion Bradford heard. She turned and sent him a smouldering look.

"More good advice?" she asked in that tense, overdefiant voice that made anything she said sound like an insult.

Roberta said quickly: "It's good of Mr. Grant to bother, Marion. He knows I know nothing about it."

Marion Bradford looked as if she would like to retort, but she merely pressed her lips together and turned back to stare out of the window. Roderick smiled at Roberta and turned his attention to his landing net. Then Ronald Beagle came out into the porch, with a rucksack on his back.

"Why," said Roberta, "Mr. Beagle's going. Are you really going up Sgurr nan Gillean in this, Mr. Beagle?"

"I think it'll clear," said Beagle. "I'm going over there anyway, and if it clears in an hour or so, as I think it will, I'll be ready." He waved vaguely to all of us, and went out into the rain.

"Well," I said to Roberta, "both the oracles have spoken, so I hope you do get your climb."

"Are you going out too?"

"My dear, I haven't even had my breakfast yet! And if I don't hurry I doubt if I'll get any!"

But as I was halfway across the hall towards the dining room I was stopped by Major Persimmon's voice calling me from the office grille. I went over. The tall, thickset countryman was still there, bending over a tray of casts, his big fingers moving them delicately.

Bill Persimmon leaned forward across the counter.

"I believe you said you wanted to hire a rod, Mrs.—er, Miss Brooke, and fish a bit?"

"Yes, I do, but I'm not quite sure when. I think I might wait a day or so, and have a look round first."

"Just as you like, of course, only—" He glanced at the other man. "If you'd really like to be shown some fishing, you might care to fix it up in advance with Dougal Macrae here. He'd be glad to go with you, I know."

The big man looked up. He had a square, brown face, deeply lined, and smallish blue eyes that looked as if, normally, they were good-tempered. Just now, they held no expression at all.

He said, in the wonderfully soft voice of the Island men: "I should be glad to show the lady how to take a fish."

"That's very good of you," I said. "Perhaps—shall we say Wednesday?"

"Wednesday iss a free day." Dougal Macrae nodded his big head. "Yess, indeed."

"Thank you very much," I said.

"Where shall I put you down for?" asked Major Persimmon.

Dougal Macrae said: "The Camasunary river, please; the upper beat. If we cannot take a fish out of there it will be a bad day indeed."

He straightened up, and picked up a well-brushed and formidable bowler hat from the office counter. "And now I must be on my way, or I shall be late at the kirk. Good day to you, mistress. Good day, Mr. Persimmon."

And he went out into the grey morning. I found myself looking after him. It had been only the most trivial of conversations, but it was my first acquaintance with the beautifully simple courtesy of the Highlander, the natural but almost royally formal bearing of the crofter who has lived all his life in the Islands. I was very much impressed with this quiet man. Dougal Macrae. Heather Macrae's father. . . .

I nodded to Major Persimmon, and went to get my belated breakfast.

I had been (rather foolishly, I suppose) dreading my next meeting with Marcia, so I was glad that she was not in the dining room. Indeed, before I had poured out my first cup of coffee, I saw a big cream-colored car come slowly past the window, and slide to a halt outside the porch door. Almost immediately, Marcia, looking enchanting and very urban in royal blue, hurried out of the hotel and was ushered into the front of the car by a handsome boy in uniform, who tucked rugs round her with solicitous care. Still in expensive and effortless silence, the car moved off.

I drank coffee, wishing I had a morning paper, so that I could pretend I hadn't noticed Nicholas who, apart from Hubert Hay, was the only other occupant of the dining room.

But it was after all the latter who in a short while rose and came over to my table.

He walked with an odd, tittuping little step that made me think again of Marcia's bouncy rubber balls, or of a self-confident robin. This latter impression was heightened by the rounded expanse of scarlet pullover which enlivened his already gay green tweeds. His face was round, too, with a small pernickety mouth, and pale blue eyes set in a multitude of radiating wrinkles. He had neat hands, and wore a big gold ring set with a black stone.

He smiled at me, showing a flash of gold in his mouth.

"Miss—er—Brooke? My name is Hay."

"How do you do?" I murmured politely.

"I hope you don't mind me coming over to speak, Miss Brooke, but the fact is"—he hesitated, and looked at me a little shyly—"the fact is, I wanted to ask a favor."

"Of course." I wondered what on earth was coming next.

"You see," he went on, still with that bashful expression that sat comically upon his round face, "you see, I'm footloose."

"You're *what?*" I said, startled.

"Footloose."

"That's what I thought you said. But—"

"It's my nom de ploom," he said. "I'm a writer." The scarlet pullover broadened perceptibly. "Footloose."

"Oh, I see! A writer—but how very clever of you, Mr. Hay. Er, novels, is it?"

"Travel books, Miss Brooke, travel books. I bring beauty to you at the fireside—that's what we put on the covers, you know. 'To you in your armchair I bring the glories of the English countryside.' And" he added, fairly, "the Scotch. That's why I'm here."

"I see. Collecting material?"

"Takin' walks," said Hubert Hay, simply. "I go on walks, and write about them, with maps. Then I mark them A, B, or C, according as to how difficult they are, and give them one, two or three stars according as to if they're pretty."

"How—very original," I said lamely, conscious of Nicholas sitting well within hearing. "It must take a lot of time."

"It's dead easy," said Hubert Hay frankly. "That is, if you can write like I can. I've always had the knack, somehow. And it pays all right."

"I shall look out for your books," I promised, and he beamed down at me.

"I'll send you one, I will indeed. The last one was called *Sauntering in Somerset.* You'd like it. And they're not *books* really, in a manner of speaking—they're paperbacks. I think the best I ever did was *Wandering through Wales.* I'll send you that too."

"Thank you very much."

I noticed then that he was holding an old *Tatler* and a *Country Life* in his hand. He put the two magazines down on the table and tapped them with a forefinger.

"I saw your photo in these," he said. "It *is* you, isn't it?"

"Yes."

He leafed through *Country Life* until he found the picture. It was me, all right, a David Gallien photograph in tweeds, with a brace of lovely Irish setters stealing the picture. Hubert Hay looked at me, all at once shy again.

"I take photos for my books," he said, hesitantly.

I waited, feeling rather helpless. Out of the corner of my eye I saw Nicholas stand up, and begin leisurely to feel in his pockets for tobacco. Hubert Hay said, with a rush: "When these geology chaps take a picture of a rock, they put a hammer in to show you the scale. I thought if I took a picture of the Coolins I'd like to—to put a lady in, so that you could tell how big the hills were, and how far away."

Nicholas was grinning. I sensed rather than saw it. Hubert Hay looked at me across David Gallien's beautifully composed advertisement, and said, wistfully: "And you do photograph nice, you do really."

Nicholas said casually: "You'd better find out what she charges. I believe it comes pretty high."

Hubert Hay looked at him, and then back at me, in a kind of naïve bewilderment. "I—shouldn't I have—?"

He looked so confused, so uncharacteristically ready to be deflated, that I forgot my own embarrassment, and Hugo Montefior's probable apoplexy. I looked furiously at Nicholas. "Mr. Drury was joking," I said swiftly. "Of course you may take a picture of me if you want to, Mr. Hay. I'd love to be in your book. When shall we do it?"

He flushed with pleasure, and the scarlet pullover expanded again to its original robin-roundness. "That's very kind of you, I'm sure, very kind indeed. I'm honored, I am really. If it clears up, how about this afternoon, on Sgurr na Stri, with the Coolins behind?"

"Fine," I said firmly.

"Bill Persimmon has a spaniel." Nicholas's voice was very bland.

"Has he?" Hubert Hay took that one happily at its face value. "Maybe that's a good idea, too. I'll go and ask him if we can borrow it."

He trotted gaily off. Nicholas stood looking down at me, still with that expression of sardonic amusement that I hated.

"What's Hugo going to say when he sees you starring

in *Staggering through Skye,* or whatever this masterpiece is going to be called?"

"He won't see it," I said tartly, as I rose. "The only traveling Hugo's interested in is Air France to Paris and back."

I started after Hubert Hay, but Nicholas moved, barring my way to the door.

"I want to talk to you, Gianetta."

I regarded him coldly. "I can't think that we have much to say to one another."

"I still want to talk to you."

"What about?"

"About us."

I raised my eyebrows. "There isn't any 'us,' Nicholas. Remember? We're not bracketed together any more. There's a separate you and a separate me, and nothing to join us together. Not even a name."

His mouth tightened. "I'm very well aware of that."

I said, before I realized what I was saying: "Was that you with Marcia Maling last night?"

His eyes flickered, and then went blank. He said: "Yes."

I walked past him out of the room.

The oracles had been right. By eleven o'clock the rain had cleared, and the clouds began to lift with startling rapidity. I saw Marion Bradford and Roberta set off up the valley about half an hour later, and, not long afterwards, Nicholas went out along the track towards Strathaird.

Shortly before noon, the sun struggled out, and, in a moment, it seemed, the sky was clear and blue, and the mist was melting from the mountain tops like snow. Sedge and heather glittered with a mass of jewels, and the frail gossamers sagged between the heather tips weighted with a Titania's ransom of diamonds.

Hubert Hay and I set out with Bill Persimmon's spaniel soon after lunch. We went down through the little birch grove to the steppingstones which spanned the Camasunary River. The birches were old and lichened, but they moved lightly in the wind, censing the bright air with raindrops, an intermittent sun-shower that we had to dodge as we took a short cut through the grove towards the river, picking our way over the wet bilberry leaves and mosses and the scattered chunks of fungus that had fallen from the trees.

We crossed the river by the steppingstones, and, after an hour or so of steep but not too difficult walking, reached the crest of Sgurr na Stri. Hubert Hay, for all his rotundity, was light on his feet, and proved, a little to my surprise, to be an entertaining companion. His knowledge and love of the countryside was not as superficial as our conversation had led me to expect; he talked knowingly of birds and deer and hill foxes, and knew, it appeared, a good deal about plants. He babbled on as he chose his "picture" and set his camera, and though he talked incessantly in clichés, I could sense that his satisfaction in what he called "the great outdoors" was deep and genuine. His resemblance to a cocky little robin became every minute more remarkable, but the quality that Marcia had called "sorbo" was, I discovered, due to an irrepressible gaiety, a delighted curiosity about everything, rather than to self-satisfaction. He was, in fact, a rather attractive little man.

We took three photographs. From the top of Sgurr na Stri you can see the whole range of the Black Cuillin, the forbidding arc that sweeps from Garsven in the south to Sgurr nan Gillean in the north, with Loch Coruisk, black as an inkwell, cupped in the roots of the mountains. I posed with the spaniel, an aristocratic but witless beast, against mountain, sky and loch in turn, while Hubert Hay fussed with his camera and darted from one point to another with little cries of polite satisfaction.

When at length he had finished we sat down together on a rock, and lit cigarettes. He seemed to have something on his mind, and smoked jerkily for a bit. Then he said:

"Miss Brooke, do you—d'you mind me saying something to you?"

"Of course not. What is it?"

"You're here alone, aren't you?"

"Yes."

His round face was worried as he looked at me earnestly. "Don't go out by yourself with anyone, Miss Brooke. You're all right with me, here, today, of course, but you weren't to know that." His rather absurd voice was somehow scarifying in its vehemence. *But don't go with anyone else.* It's not safe."

I said nothing for a moment. I realized that I had, actually, since breakfast that morning, forgotten the sort of danger that was walking these hills.

"You don't mind me saying?" asked Hubert Hay anxiously.

"Of course not. You're perfectly right. I promise you I'll be careful." There was a certain irony about the admonition, repeating as it did Roderick Grant's warning of the night before. Could I, then, eliminate two of the suspects among the "gentlemen from the hotel," or were these warnings some subtle kind of double bluff? If I went on going for walks with the "gentlemen," no doubt I should find out soon enough. I shivered a little, and pulled the dog's ears. "It's not a very pleasant thought, is it?"

His face flushed dark red. "It's damnable! I—I beg your pardon, I'm sure. But that's the only word I can think of. Miss Brooke"—he turned to me with a queer, almost violent gesture—"that girl, Heather Macrae—she was only eighteen!"

I said nothing.

"It was her birthday." His funny high little voice held a note almost of savagery. "Her eighteenth birthday." He took a pull at his cigarette, and then spoke more calmly: "I feel it a bit, Miss Brooke. You see, I knew her."

"You knew her? Well?"

"Oh dear no. Only to speak to, as you might say. I'd stopped at the croft a couple of times, when I was out walking, and she'd made me a pot of tea. She was a pretty girl, gay and a bit cheeky, and kind of full of life. There wasn't a bit of badness in her. Nothing to ask for—what she got."

"*You* didn't get any hint as to who she going with?" It was a silly question, of course, as the police would have gone over the ground with meticulous thoroughness, but he answered without impatience: "No, none at all."

But his voice had altered subtly, so that I glanced at him. "You got *something?*"

"A very little hint," he said carefully. "I told her that I was writing a book, of course, and she was interested. People usually are. . . . She said that quite a lot of folks came around the crofts, one way or another, asking questions about local customs and superstitions and the like. I asked her if she had any special superstitions—just joking-like—and she said no, of course not, she was a modern girl. Then I said wasn't there any magic still going on in the Islands like there used to be, and"—he turned pale round eyes on me—"she shut up like an oyster, and pretty near hustled me out of the kitchen."

"Magic?" I said. "But that's absurd!"

He nodded. "I know. But, you know, I can't help having a feeling about this murder. It must have been all *planned,* you see. The stuff he'd used for the bonfire must have been taken up there, bit by bit, quite deliberately. There was heather and peat and branches of birchwood, and a big chunk of oak hardly charred, and a lot of that dry fungus— agaric—that you get on birch trees."

I made an exclamation, but he hadn't heard me. "Then, when he is ready, he gets the girl up there. . . . Just think a minute, if you'll excuse me bringing it up again . . . the fire, and the shoes and things in a neat pile, all tidy, and the girl laid out with her throat cut and her hands crossed, and ashes on her face. . . . Why, it's like a—a *sacrifice!*"

The last word came out with a jerk. I was on my feet staring down at him, with my spine prickling.

"But that's *crazy!*"

The pale, troubled eyes glanced up. "That's just it, isn't it? Whoever did it must be just plain crazy. And he looks and acts just as sane as you or me . . . except sometimes." He got to his feet and regarded me solemnly. "So I would- n't go for walks with anybody, if I was you."

"I won't" I said fervently. "In fact, I'm beginning to think that I might go back to London, after all."

"It wouldn't be a bad idea, at that," said he, picking up his camera, and turning to follow me down the hill.

Chapter 8

I WAS STILL WONDERING IF IT WOULDN'T, after all, be wis- est to leave the hotel, when something happened that made me decide, at any rate for the time being, that I must stay.

It was in the lounge, after dinner, that the first stirring of a new uneasiness began to make itself plain. Alastair Braine, carrying coffee cups, paused in the middle of the room and said, on a slight note of surprise: "Hullo, aren't the climbers back yet?"

"They weren't at dinner," said Alma Corrigan.

Colonel Cowdray-Simpson said: "Good God, neither were they. I hope there's nothing amiss."

"That fool woman!" said Mrs. Cowdray-Simpson, roundly. "She shouldn't have gone up on a day like this."

Alastair said reassuringly: "I shouldn't worry. They've probably only gone a little farther than they meant to, and after all, it's still light."

Nicholas looked up from a letter he was writing. "The weather was clearing nicely when they went, and there's been no mist on Blaven this afternoon. They'll be all right."

"If only," said Marcia Maling, "if only that *awful* woman hasn't gone and done something silly, just to impress! That *poor* child Roberta—"

Roderick Grant said quietly: "Miss Bradford is actually a very accomplished climber. She wouldn't take any risks with a beginner. And Drury is quite right about the weather. After all, Ronald Beagle went up Sgurr nan Gillean, and he certainly wouldn't have gone if it hadn't been all right."

"He's not back either," said Hubert Hay.

There was a little silence. I sensed discomfort and uneasiness growing.

"Neither is he," said Alma Corrigan, rather stupidly. "Well, I suppose—"

"Where's your husband?" asked Mrs. Cowdray-Simpson.

The question sounded abrupt, but there was nothing in it to make Alma Corrigan flush scarlet, as she did. "He—he went out walking."

She was so obviously embarrassed that everybody else began to feel embarrassed too, without knowing the reason. Alastair said quickly: "We all went out after lunch to walk up to the ridge for the view over Loch Slapin. I brought Mrs. Corrigan back, but Hart went farther."

"Oh, you went that way? Did you see the women, then, on Blaven?" asked Colonel Cowdray-Simpson.

"Not a sign. We saw someone—I believe it was Drury— in the distance, but not another living soul."

"I wasn't on Blaven," said Nicholas, "so I didn't see them either."

Roderick Grant put down his coffee cup and got to his feet. "It's only eight-thirty, and I don't personally think we need to worry yet, but they certainly should have got back by this. I think I'll have a word with Bill. They may have told him if they were going to be late."

He went quickly into the hall, where I could see him leaning over the office counter, in earnest conversation with Major Persimmon.

"Sensible chap," said Colonel Cowdray-Simpson. "No point in our starting a fuss."

But Marcia was not to be stopped so easily. "This is *too* ghastly, isn't it? What d'you suppose *could* have happened to them?"

"Plenty of things can happen in the Cuillin," said Alma Corrigan, rather tartly, "and altogether too many things *have* been happening lately."

"*That* affair?" said Alastair. "That can hardly have any connection—"

"I'm not talking about the murder," said Alma brutally. I heard Marcia give a little gasp. "I'm talking about climbing accidents." She looked round the circle of faces, her fine eyes serious and a little frightened. "Do you realize how many people have been killed by the Cuillin, this year alone?"

Her use of the preposition gave the sentence an oddly macabre twist, and I saw Marcia glance over her shoulder to where the great hills towered against the massed clouds of evening "Is it—a lot?" She sounded a little awe-stricken.

"Four," said Alma Corrigan, and added, almost absently, "so far. . . ."

I felt the little cold caress of fear along the back of my neck, and was grateful for the Colonel's brisk interposition. "Well," he said, practically, "if people will go wandering out in these mountains with only the haziest ideas about how to climb them, they must expect accidents. In almost every case these mishaps are brought about by ignorance or carelessness, and I'm sure we can acquit Beagle and Miss Bradford on both these grounds. We're making an unnecessary fuss, and I think we'd better stop talking about it and frightening ourselves."

He turned to Alastair with some remark about tomorrow's sport, and in a few minutes tension seemed to be relieved, and people were chatting generally.

I turned to Marcia Maling. "Where did you go today?"

"To Portree, my dear"—her face lit up with the familiar warm *gamine* charm—"along the most *ghastly* roads, with poor dear Fergus snarling like a tomcat all the way because he'd just washed the car."

"I thought there was an excellent road from Broadford?"

"Oh, there is. But it goes *snaking* about with the most *ghastly* hairpin bends and cliffs and things—"

"But, Marcia, the views—"

The views were dismissed with a wave of her cigarette. "It was divine, of course," she said quickly, "only it was raining. And then Portree on Sunday is the utter *end*. But I got some marvellous tweed there on Friday. I'll show it to you tonight. It's a sort of misty purple, and quite gorgeous."

But here Roderick came back into the lounge, and there was a lull in the conversation as eyes turned towards him.

"Bill Persimmon says there's no earthly reason to worry," he said reassuringly, but, as he crossed the room towards me, I though I saw uneasiness in the glance he cast at the sky outside.

Someone switched on the radio, and the lugubrious weather report insinuated itself into the conversation. Colonel Cowdray-Simpson moved nearer to listen.

"Waiting for news of Everest," said Roderick to me with a grin. "That, with the notable absence of fish in the rivers, seems to be the Colonel's main preoccupation."

"He's rather sweet," I said. "I'd hate him to be disappointed, but, you know, I have the oddest feeling about Everest. . . . I believe I'd be almost sorry to see it climbed."

"Sorry?" He looked at me curiously. "Why on earth?"

I laughed. "Not really, I suppose. But I'd always imagined it as the last inviolate spot that arrogant man hadn't smeared himself over, sort of remote and white and unattainable. Immaculate, that's the word I want. I somehow think it would be a pity to see man's footmarks in the snow."

"I didn't know you were a poet, Gianetta," said Nicholas's voice above me, lazily mocking. He had come over to the window just behind my chair.

I felt myself flushing, and Roderick looked a little annoyed.

"Why should you? I didn't know you knew Miss Brooke."

His voice was curt. Nicholas eyed him for a moment.

"Why should you?" he echoed, unpleasantly, and turned away to the window. "And here, if I'm not mistaken, is our friend Beagle at last."

"Alone?" asked Mrs. Cowdray-Simpson.

"Yes . . . that's odd."

"What's odd?" asked Alastair, joining him.

"He's coming down the glen from Loch na Creitheach. I thought he went up Sgurr nan Gillean," said Nicholas thoughtfully. "Wouldn't it have been easier for him to come down the west side of the glen and over the stepping-stones?"

"There's nothing in it," said Alastair. "That's a shorter way, certainly, but the going's terrible, while there's a path down the Blaven side of Creitheach."

Roderick said: "He may have seen the two women, if he's come along the glen. It's still light enough to see some-one on the south ridge."

But Beagle, when he came in, denied that he had seen anyone. And the worried look that came over his face when he heard that the two girls were still out, brought back with a rush the apprehensions that we had been try-ing to dismiss. He went to change and eat a late meal, and we all sat, talking in fits and starts, and trying not to look out of the window too often, for another half hour of steadily mounting anxiety.

By half past nine it was pretty dark. Rain clouds had massed in great indigo banks right across the sky, shutting out any speck of residual light that might linger in the west. Wisps of wet mist scudded underneath the higher cloud, and the fingers of the gusty wind clawed at the win-dows, flinging rain in spasmodic handfuls against the glass. By now everybody, I think, was convinced that something had happened to the two women, and it was almost a relief when, at nine thirty exactly, Bill Persim-mon came into the lounge and said, without preamble:

"I think we'd better go out and look for them. Mr. Cor-rigan has just come in with Dougal, and they say there's still no sign of them coming down the glen."

The men were on their feet.

"You're sure they went up Blaven?"

Persimmon said: "Certain. They—"

"They might have changed their minds," said Nicholas.

Bill Persimmon looked at him, queerly, I thought. He said slowly: "They went to Blaven, all right. They were seen on it."

"Seen?" said Roderick. "When? Whereabouts?"

"At the Sputan Dhu," said Persimmon dryly.

Ronald Beagle started forward. "At the—but *my God,*

man, that's no place for a beginner! The Black Spout! That's a devilish tricky climb. Are you sure, Persimmon?"

We all stared at Bill Persimmon, while our imagined fears gradually assumed a horrible reality.

"Who saw them?" asked Nicholas quickly.

Bill looked at him again. "Dougal Macrae. He saw them making for the gully at about four o'clock. All three of them."

My throat was suddenly dry. I heard myself say in a strange voice: "All *three* of them?"

He nodded and his eyes went round the group of faces where a new sort of fear was beginning to dawn. He said: "Dougal says there were three. And . . . everybody else is back. Odd, isn't it?"

"Perhaps they had a guide," said Nicholas.

"They set out without one," said Roderick.

Bill Persimmon backed to the swing door, thrusting it open with his shoulder. "We'll discuss it after we've found them and brought them in," he said. "The ladies would be well advised to stay indoors. Will the men be ready in five minutes? Come along to the kitchen then, and my wife'll have sandwiches and coffee ready."

I got up. "Can't we help there?"

"That would be very good of you, ma'am. I expect she'd be glad of a hand."

Then he pushed through the door with the other men after him.

When, at length, they had all gone out into the gusty dark, I went slowly back to the lounge. I was thinking, not very coherently, about Dougal Macrae's story. Three climbers? *Three*?

There could be no possible connection, of course—but I found myself wondering what Jamesy Farlane looked like.

Alma Corrigan had gone to bed, and Mrs. Cowdray-Simpson was upstairs with her mother-in-law. Marcia and I were alone again in the lounge. The curtains had been drawn to shut out the storm, but the rain was hurtling against the windows in fistfuls, and the wind sounded vicious. Behind its spasmodic bursts of violence droned the steady sound of the sea.

Marcia shivered, and stretched her legs to the fire. Her eyes looked big and scared.

"Isn't this too utterly ghastly?" she said, and through the outworn extravagance of the phrase I could hear the strain plucking at her throat.

"I'm afraid it does look as if something had happened," I said. "Look, I brought us both a drink, Marcia."

"Oh, you angel." She took the glass and drank a generous mouthful. "My God, I needed that!" She leaned forward in her chair. The big eyes seemed bigger than ever. "Janet, do you believe there *is* a hoodoo on the mountain?"

I gave a laugh that was probably not very convincing. "No, of course not. They just went climbing in too hard a place and got stuck. It's always happening. They'll turn up all right."

"But—the other climber?"

"Whoever it was," I said robustly, "it certainly wasn't a ghost."

She gave a little sigh. "Well, the quicker they're found the sooner to sleep. I hope to heaven nothing's happened to that Roberta child. She's rather sweet—pathetic, in a way. I wonder—"

"It was the other one I found pathetic," I said, and then realized with a shock that I had spoken in the past tense.

But Marcia had not noticed. "That ghastly Bradford woman? But, my dear, she *is impossible*! Not that I'd want anything to happen to her, but really—!"

"She must be a very unhappy woman," I said, "to be like that. She must know she's making everybody dislike her, and yet some devil inside her drives her perpetually to antagonize everyone she meets."

"Frustrated," said Marcia cruelly, *"and* how. She's in love with Roderick Grant."

I set my glass down with a click, and spoke almost angrily. "Marcia! That's absurd!"

She giggled. She looked like a very pretty cat. "It is not. Haven't you seen the way she looks at him?"

I said sharply: "Don't talk nonsense. She was abominably rude to him, both last night and this morning. I heard her."

"Uh-huh," said Marcia, on a rising note of mockery. "All the same, you watch the way she looks at him. It's just about as noticeable as the way he *doesn't* look at her —just looks down his nose in that charming well-bred way he has, and then jumps at the chance of taking *you* for a walk! If I were you, darling, I'd keep out of her range."

"Oh, nonsense," I said again, feeling horribly uncomfortable. I got up. "I think I'll go to bed."

Marcia uncurled herself, and drained her glass. "I'll come too. I'm certainly not going to sit down here alone. I imagine we'll hear them coming back, and'll find out what's happened then."

She linked her arm in mine as we went up the stairs, and grinned at me. "Annoyed with me?"

"Of course not. Why should I be?"

"Honey, on account of I say things I oughtn't. And that reminds me—I'm afraid I gave you away tonight. I didn't mean to."

"Gave me away? What d'you mean?"

"I let out to Roderick Grant that you and Nicky had been divorced. I forget how it came up—it was during the shemozzle tonight, when you were in the kitchen. I'm sorry, truly I am."

"It's all right." Nicky, I thought. Nicky. I'll bet she spells it Nikki. . . .

"I hope it doesn't matter," said Marcia.

I laughed. "Why should it? I don't suppose he'll tell anyone else."

"Oh, well. . . ." We had reached the stairhead. *"That's* all right, then. Come and see my tweed before you go to bed."

I followed her along the passage to her room. The window at the end showed, tonight, only a square of roaring grey against which our reflections glimmered, distorted and pale. Marcia pushed her door open and went in, groping for the light switch.

"Just a sec., I'll see—" The light went on.

I heard her gasp. She was standing as if frozen, her back to me, her hands up to her throat.

Then she screamed, a high, tearing scream.

For a paralyzed, horrified moment I couldn't move. My body turned to ice and I stood there, without breath.

Then she screamed again, and whirled round to face me, one hand flung out in a gesture of terror, the other clutching her throat.

I moved then. I jumped forward and seized the hand. I said: "Marcia, for God's sake, what is it?"

Her breath came roughly, in gasps. *"The murderer. Oh my God, the murderer. . . ."*

"Marcia, there's no one here."

She was shaking violently. She grabbed my arm and held it tightly. She pointed to the bed, her lips shaking so much that she couldn't speak coherently.

I stared down at the bed, while the slow goose flesh pricked up my spine.

Lying on the coverlet was a doll, the kind of frivolous doll in a flounced skirt that the Marcias of this world love to have sprawling about on divans and sofas among the satin cushions. I had seen dozens of them—flaxen-headed, blue-eyed, pink and white and silken.

But this one was different.

It was lying flat on its back on the bed, with its legs straight out and its hands crossed on its breast. The contents of an ash tray had been scattered over it, and a great red gash gleamed across its neck, where its throat was cut from ear to ear.

Chapter 9

THEY FOUND NO TRACE, that night, of either Marion Bradford or Roberta.

The night had been black and wild, and after several fruitless and exhausting hours of climbing and shouting in the blustering darkness, the searchers had straggled home in the early hours of daylight, to snatch food and a little sleep before setting out, haggard-eyed and weary, for a further search. Bill Persimmon had telephoned for the local rescue team, and, at about nine the next morning, a force some twenty strong set out once again for what must now certainly be reckoned the scene of an accident.

This time, I went with them. Even if I couldn't rock-climb, I would at least provide another pair of eyes, and I could help to cover some of the vast areas of scree and rough heather bordering the Black Spout.

The morning—I remembered with vague surprise that it was the eve of Coronation Day—had broken grey and forbidding. The wind still lurched among the cairns and heather braes with inconsequent violence, and the frequent showers of rain were arrow-sharp and heavy. We were all muffled to the eyes, and trudged our way up the sodden glen with heads bent to meet the vicious stabbing of the rain.

It was a little better as we came under the shelter of the hill where Roderick and I had talked two nights ago, but, as we struggled on to the crest of it, the wind met us again in force. The raindrops drove like nails before it, and I turned my back to it for a moment's respite. The storm gust leaped past me, wrenching at my coat, and fled down the valley towards the sea.

The hotel looked far away and small and lonely, with, behind it, the sea loch whitening under the racing feet of the wind. I saw a car move slowly away from the porch, and creep along the storm-lashed track to Strathaird. It was a big car, cream, with a black convertible top.

"Marcia Maling's car," said a voice at my elbow. It was Alma Corrigan, looking businesslike in Burberry and scarlet scarf and enormous nailed boots. She looked also, I noticed, decidedly attractive, now that the wind had whipped red into her cheeks and a sparkle into her fine eyes. She added, with a touch of contempt, as we turned to make our way along the top of the spur: "I suppose it would be too much to expect her to come along as well, but she needn't have taken the chauffeur away with her. Every man we can get—"

"She's leaving," I said.

She checked in her stride. "Leaving? You mean going home?"

"Yes. She's going back to London. She told me so last night."

"But I thought she planned to stay a week at least! I suppose this affair, on top of the other business—"

"I suppose so," I said, noncommittally. I was certainly not going to tell anyone the reason for Marcia's sudden decision. Mrs. Persimmon knew, and Mrs. Cowdray-Simpson, but if Marcia's hysterics had not disturbed Alma Corrigan the night before, so much the better. And I was more than ever certain that I, myself, was going home tomorrow. But since I had not, like Marcia, been, so to speak, warned away, I felt I could hardly go without finding out what had happened to Marion and Roberta.

"Well!" said Mrs. Corrigan, on an odd note which was

three parts relief and one of something else I could not identify. "I can't pretend I'm brokenhearted to see her go. She's only been here five days, and"—she broke off and sent me a sidelong glance up from under her long lashes—"you'd understand how I feel, if you were a married woman, Miss Brooke."

"No doubt." I added gently: "She couldn't help it, you know. . . . She's been spoiled, I suppose, and she *is* such a lovely creature."

"You're more charitable than I am," said Alma Corrigan, a little grimly. "But then, you haven't so much to lose."

I didn't pretend to misunderstand her. "She had to have men's admiration," I said, "all the time, no matter who got hurt in the process. I—forgive me, but I'd put it behind you, if I were you. Can't you begin to pretend it never happened?"

She laughed a little, hardly. "It's easy to see you don't know much about dealing with men."

I didn't speak for a moment. I wondered irritably why married women so often adopted that tone, almost of superior satisfaction in the things they had to suffer. Then I told myself that she was probably right. I had after all failed utterly to deal with the man I had married, so who was I to give her advice? I thought wryly that nobody ever wanted advice anyway; all that most people sought was a ratification of their own views.

We were passing the Coronation bonfire, and I changed the subject. "I suppose they'll hardly light that bonfire now. I mean, celebrations won't exactly be in keeping, if anything's happened to these two girls."

She said morosely: "The sticks'll be wet, anyway," and added, with the determined gloom of a mouse returning to its accustomed treadmill: "But how can Hart just expect to go on the way he has? He's been following her round like a lap dog, making a fool of me, ever since she came. Oh, you haven't seen much of it. She switched to that Drury man last night, but *really*—I mean, *everybody* must have noticed. It's all very well saying she can't help it, but what about Hart? Why should Hart be allowed to get away with that sort of thing? I've a damned good mind to—"

I said abruptly: "Do you want to keep your husband or don't you?"

"I—of course I want to keep him! What a silly question!"

"Then leave him alone," I said. "Don't you know yet that there's no room for pride in marriage? You have to choose between the two. If you can't keep quiet, then you must make up your mind to lose him. If you want *him*, then swallow your pride and shut up. It'll heal over; everything does, given time enough and a bit of peace."

She opened her mouth, probably to ask me what I knew about it anyway.

"We're getting left behind," I said, almost roughly. "Let's hurry."

I broke away from her and forged ahead up the rapidly steepening path.

We had climbed to a good height already, and I was thankful to notice, as we began to thread our way up the deer tracks on the westerly flanks of Blaven itself, that the force of the wind was lessening. The gusts were less frequent and less violent, and, by the time we had reached the base of the first scree slopes, the rain had stopped, shut off as suddenly as if by the turning of a tap.

The party was strung out now in single file, forging at a steeply climbing angle along the mountainside. Most of the men carried packs; several had coils of rope. The going got harder; the deer paths narrowed and steepened. These were foot-wide depressions—no more—in the knee-deep heather, and they were treacherous with the rain. Occasionally we found ourselves having to skirt great outcrops of rock, clinging precariously to roots and tufts of heather, with our feet slithering, slipping on the narrow ledge of mud which was all that remained of the path.

Above us towered the enormous cliffs of the south ridge, gleaming-black with rain, rearing steeply out of the precipitous scree like a roach-backed monster from the waves. The scree itself was terrifying enough. It fell away from the foot of the upper cliffs, hundreds of feet of fallen stone, slippery and overgrown and treacherous with hidden holes and loose rocks, which looked as if a false step might bring half the mountainside down in one murderous avalanche.

The place where Dougal Macrae had seen the climbers was about halfway along Blaven's western face. There the crest of the mountain stands up above the scree in an enormous hogback of serrated peaks, two thousand feet and more of grim and naked rock, shouldering up the scudding sky. I stopped and looked up. Streams of wind-torn mist raced and broke round the buttresses of the dreadful rock; against its sheer precipices the driven clouds wrecked themselves in swirls of smoke; and, black and terrible, above the movement of the storm, behind the racing riot of grey cloud, loomed and vanished and loomed again the great devil's pinnacles that broke the sky and split the winds into streaming rack. Blaven flew its storms like a banner.

And from some high black corrie among the peaks spilled the tiny trickle of water that was to form the gully of the Sputan Dhu. I could just see it, away up on some remote and fearful face of rock—a thin white line, no more, traced across the grey, a slender, steady line that seemed not to move at all save when the force of the wind took it and made it waver a little, like gossamer in the breeze. And the slowly falling gossamer line of white water had cut, century by century, deep into the living rock, slashing a dark fissure for itself down the side of the mountain. Through this it slid, and rushed, and slid again, now hidden, now leaping clear, but all the time growing and loudening and gathering force until it reached the lowest pitch of the mountain and sank clamorously out of sight in the cleft that split the upper edge of the precipice above the scree.

And then at last it sprang free of the mountain. From the base of the cleft, some hundred feet up the face, it leaped as from a gutterspout, a narrow jet of roaring water that jumped clear of the rock to plunge the last hundred feet in one sheer white leap of foam. And then it vanished into the loud depths of the gully it had bitten through the scree.

Up the edge of this gully the rescue party slowly picked its way. At intervals, someone shouted, but the only answer was the bark of a startled raven, which wheeled out from the cliff above, calling hoarsely among the mocking echoes.

I clawed my way over the wet rocks, my shoes slipping on slimy tufts of grass and thrift, my breath coming in uneven gasps, my face damp and burning with exertion in spite of the intermittent buffets of the chill wet wind. The men forged steadily ahead, their seemingly careless slouch covering the ground at a remarkable speed. I clambered and gasped in their wake, lifting my eyes oc-

casionally to the menace of those black cliffs ahead that
rode, implacably grim and remote, above the flying tails
of the storm. Down to our left, at the bottom of the gully,
the water brawled and bellowed and swirled in its devil's
potholes. Here was a veritable demon's cleft; a black
fissure, seventy feet deep, bisecting the scree slope, its walls
were sheer, black and dripping, its floor a mass of boulders and wrestling water.

Suddenly, and for the first time clearly, I realized that
somewhere here, in this wilderness of cruel rock and
weltering water, two young women were probably lying
dead. Or, at best, alive and maimed and unable, above the
intermittent roar of wind and water, to make themselves
heard.

I found myself repeating, breathlessly, stupidly, in a
whisper: "Roberta . . . Roberta. . . ."

The man directly in front of me was Alastair. He
turned and gave me a quick, reassuring smile, and reached
out a big hand to steady me up the slope.

"Don't go too near the edge, Janet . . . that's better.
We'll soon get them now, if Dougal was right. These
rescue chaps know every inch of the place, you know."

"But . . . Alastair"—exertion had made me only half
articulate—"they can't be alive still. They must have—
must be—"

"If they managed to creep into shelter, they could quite
easily be alive, providing they weren't seriously hurt by
a fall. It wasn't cold last night."

"Do you believe there were three of them?"

"Dougal Macrae isn't exactly given to flights of fancy,"
said Alastair.

"Are any of the local men missing?"

"I'm told not."

"Then, if there *were* three people, the third climber
must be someone from the hotel. And nobody's missing
from there either."

"Exactly so," said Alastair, in a blank noncommittal sort
of voice.

"And if nobody from the hotel reported the accident,
then it means—"

"Exactly so," said Alastair again. He paused and took
my arm. Then with his free hand he pointed upwards,
and a little to the right of where we were standing.

"That's where the bonfire was, that night," he said. Then he dropped my arm and addressed himself to the climb again.

I followed, numbly. Murder? Again? Who on earth would want to murder Marion and Roberta? It was absurd. But then what reason could there have been for the murder of Heather Macrae—and such a murder? But again (I told myself) between the two incidents there could be no possible similarity. The disappearance of two climbers was, if not normal, at any rate not tainted with the fantastic, almost ritual air of the other death. Or was it? When we found the bodies. . . .

I pushed the wet hair back from my face with an unsteady hand, and looked up.

The men ahead had stopped climbing, and were gathered on the edge of the gully at the point where the waterfall leaped its final hundred feet or so from the upper cliff. Someone was pointing downwards. Ropes were being uncoiled.

I hauled myself up the last step of rock and paused. Then I walked slowly forward to join them.

I was afraid, horribly afraid. I felt that no power on earth would make me look down over that edge of rock to see Roberta staring up at me with sightless eyes, with her throat cut like that of Marcia's silken doll, and the bright blood splashed into pink by the rain, crawling between the clumps of blossoming thrift.

But it appeared that no sign of either Roberta or Marion had yet been seen, though anxious eyes scanned the depths of the black gully. Dougal Macrae pointed out to the rest of the men the place where he had seen the climbers—he had not, it is true, seen them actually on the cliff, but they were making for it at an angle which suggested that they intended either to climb on the face of the Spout itself or to cross above the fall by the upper rocks.

Roderick Grant turned his head and saw me, and came over, tugging a battered pack of cigarettes from some inner pocket. He handed me one, and we lit up—no easy process this, as the force of the gusty wind had not appreciably diminished.

"What are they going to do?" I asked anxiously.

"If Dougal's right, and they were starting to climb across

the Spout, then the first move is to do the same climb.
There may be some traces in the rocks above the gully,
or the climbers may be able to see down below the fall."

"Did you get this far last night?"

"Yes, but of course it was no use in the dark. All we
could do was shout."

I looked down into the cleft, where the white water
leaped and wrangled. The sides of the gully gleamed and
dripped, the hanging tufts of fern and heather tossing in
the currents of wind that roared up the cleft like air in a
wind tunnel. With each gust the water of the fall was
blown back, and flattened in its own spray against the
rock. The echo was uncanny.

I shivered, and then looked up again at the grim pitch
above us. "Is it a very bad place to climb?"

He was grave. "It's pretty bad for anyone, and for a
beginner it's—well, it's sheer lunacy."

"Can the men get down into the gully if they—if they
have to?" I asked fearfully.

"Oh, yes. Beagle says he'll go, and Rhodri MacDowell
is going with him. He's a local chap and a pretty good
climber."

I peered down again into the echoing depths. "Doesn't
the gully flatten out farther down the mountain? I mean,
couldn't they start down there, and work their way up
the bottom of it?"

"This is quicker. It would take hours to work up from
below. The stream goes down in leaps, you see—anything
from seven to twenty feet at a time. It's much simpler to
go straight down here."

Operations were beginning at the foot of the cliff. Three
of the men, of whom Beagle was one, were roping themselves together, preparatory to making the climb across
the Spout. The rest of the group had split up, and small
parties of men seemed to be casting back along the hillside, among the smaller clefts and fissures in the scree.

"What do we do?" I asked Roderick.

"I should wait here. If they do find them, injured, you
might be able to help." He smiled at me reassuringly. "The
odds aren't quite as bad as they look, Janet. It won't be
long before we have them safely back at the hotel."

Then he was gone, and I was left with Alma Corrigan
and the little group of men who remained to watch the
climb across the gully.

Chapter 10

I DON'T PRETEND TO KNOW ANYTHING about the art of rock-climbing. The three men who were climbing out across the face of the Sputan Dhu were all, it appeared, experts at the job; and indeed, they moved so easily and smoothly on the rock that it was hard to believe the traverse was as dangerous as Roderick had made out.

I had gone farther up the scree to a point near the start of the climb, and sat, watching and nervously smoking, while the three climbers moved steadily, turn and turn about, across the wet cliff. The route they followed took them at a steep angle up the rock face, at one point straddling the narrow cleft above the spout of water. Even to my ignorant eyes it was obvious that the wet rock and gusty wind must add considerably to the risks of the climb, but the climbers appeared unaffected by the conditions. Ronald Beagle was first on the rope, leading with a smooth precision that was beautiful to watch. The other two, Rhodri MacDowell and a lad called Iain, were members of the local rescue team. All three—it seemed to me—took the climb very slowly, with long pauses between each man's move, when, I imagine, they were looking for traces of the other climbers. They gave no sign, however, of having found any, but moved on, unhurriedly, up and across the dreadful gap.

Dougal Macrae said, just behind me: "That's a bonny climber."

Ronald Beagle was halfway up what looked like a perpendicular slab of gleaming rock—a hideously exposed pitch, as the slab was set clear above the gully. He climbed rhythmically and easily, making for the next stance, which was an intilted ledge some fifteen feet above him.

"I think he's wonderful," I said warmly. "I don't know anything about climbing, but it looks uncommonly tricky to me."

"It's a fery nasty place," said Dougal. "And that bit that Mr. Beagle is on now—that is the worst."

"It looks like it."

"He must be right out over the gully. Ah, he's up. He's belaying now."

Beagle had swung himself easily onto the ledge, and was busy looping himself in some way to a jut of rock beside him. Then he turned and called down something to the men below. I couldn't hear what it was, but he must have been telling them to wait, for neither of them moved from their stances. Beagle turned to face outwards and, crouching in the support of the belayed rope, he bent to peer down into the gully.

I cried out involuntarily: "But they can't be down there, Mr. Macrae! It's impossible!"

He looked somberly down over his pipe. "If they fell from yon piece of rock that's where they'll be."

"That's what I mean." I fumbled with chilled fingers for another cigarette. "They'd never have crossed that piece of rock. That girl, Roberta Symes—she'd never have tackled a climb like that. She'd never climbed before!"

His brows drew down. "D'ye say so?"

"That's what she told us. And Miss Bradford was apparently a good climber. She'd never have let Roberta try this route—surely she wouldn't!"

"No. You'd think not." He raised troubled eyes again to the dangerous pitch. "No. But it was for this place they were making when I saw them. It did look indeed as if they were planning to cross the Sputan Dhu—ah, they've moved again."

Rhodri MacDowell, the middle man, was now on Beagle's ledge, while Beagle himself was out of sight round an overhang which beetled over the far side of the gully. Iain, who was last on the rope, was moving up.

I dragged on my cigarette with a nervous movement, and shifted on the wet stone. "I—I wonder if they've seen anything—down there?" The words, tremulous and reluctant, were snatched into nothing by the wet wind.

"We'll hope ye're right, and that they'd never let the lassie try the place. It may be—"

"They?" I turned on him quickly. "It was you who said there were three climbers, wasn't it? I suppose you couldn't have made a mistake, could you? You're really sure about it?"

"Oh, aye." The soft voice was decisive. "There were three, sure enough."

"And the third one—was it a man or a woman?"

"I don't know. At that distance I could not tell very much about them, and nowadays all the ladies wear trousers on the hill, it seems. There was not anything I could be picking out, except that the middle one had a red jacket on."

"That would be Miss Symes," I said, and remembered with a pang how the scarlet windbreaker had suited Roberta's bright Dutch-doll face and black hair.

"It would make it easy enough to find her now, you'd think," said Dougal.

"I—I suppose so." The second climber had disappeared now. The rope gleamed in a pale penciled line across the overhang to where Iain was working his way up to the ledge. He gained it presently, and belayed. I heard him call something and soon Ronald Beagle reappeared some way beyond him, making for what looked like the end of the climb, a widish ledge above the scree at the far side of the gully, from which the descent was only an easy scramble.

In a very few minutes more all three climbers had foregathered on the ledge, and seemed to be holding some sort of a conference. The people on our side of the gully, Alma Corrigan, Dougal Macrae, myself, and the handful of men who had not gone to search the scree slopes, watched in stony silence, frozen into a dismal set piece of foreboding. I sat there with my forgotten cigarette burning one-sidedly between wet fingers, stupidly straining eyes and ears to interpret the distant sounds and gestures of the men's conversation.

Dougal said suddenly: "I think they must have seen something in the gully."

"No," I said, and then again, foolishly, as if I could somehow push the truth further away from me, "no."

"Rhodri MacDowell is pointing. I thought he had seen something when he was on the cliff."

I blinked against the wet wind, and saw that one of the men was, indeed, gesturing back towards the gully. The three of them had disengaged themselves from the rope, and now began to make a rapid way down the scree towards the far side of the gully. There was about them a purposeful air that gave Dougal's guess the dismal ring of truth.

Then Alma Corrigan turned abruptly from the little group nearby, and strode across to us.

"They're down there," she announced baldly.

I just stared at her, unable to speak, but I got stiffly to my feet. Behind her the hotel proprietor, Bill Persimmon, said quickly: "We don't know for certain, but it does seem as if they've seen something."

"Ye'll be going down the gully then," said Dougal Macrae.

"I suppose so." Bill Persimmon turned back to watch the climbers' approach.

Behind us we heard the rasp and slither of boots on wet heather. Nicholas came down the slope, with Roderick not far in the rear. Nicholas's eyes, narrowed against the rain, were intent on Beagle as he approached the opposite side of the gully.

"It's time someone else took a turn," he said abruptly. "If they've been seen in the gully, I'll go down. What about you, Bill?"

"I think," began Major Persimmon, "that perhaps we ought—"

"Did they see anything down there?" Roderick's voice cut anxiously across his. "We came back because it looked as if—we thought—" He saw my face, and stopped; then he came over quickly to stand beside me, giving me a little smile of reassurance.

But I shook my head at it. "I'm afraid they did," I said under my breath. "Dougal says one of the men saw something."

"Yes. Rhodri. We saw him pointing. I'm very much afraid—" He stopped again, and bit his underlip. "Why don't you go back to the hotel, Janet?"

"Good Lord," I said, almost savagely, "don't worry about *me*. *I'm* all right."

And now the three climbers were at the edge of the gully. Beagle's voice came gustily across the fitful noises of wind and water.

". . . Below the pool . . . couldn't really see . . . might be . . . a leg . . . going down now. . . ."

I sat down again, rather suddenly, on my stone. I think I was surprised that, now it had happened, I felt no horror, only numbness. The small things—the sluggish misery of wet shoes, the chilly drizzle, my handkerchief sodden in my coat pocket—each petty detail of discomfort seemed in turn to nag at my attention, and fix it, dazedly, upon myself. I suppose it is one kind of automatic defense; it may be a variety of shock; at any rate I just sat there, dumbly working my fingers into my damp gloves, while all round me preparations were made for the final horror of discovery.

Beagle and Rhodri MacDowell went down after all. To me, watching them with that same detached, almost childish interest, it seemed an amazing operation. They were so incredibly quick. Beagle was still shouting his information across the gully when Rhodri and the lad Iain had thrown the rope over a little pylon of rock that jutted up beside them. The ends of the doubled rope snaked down into the depths, touched bottom, and hung there. Rhodri said something to Iain, heaved the rope somehow between his legs and over his shoulder, and then simply walked backwards over the cliff. He backed down it rapidly, leaning out, as it were, against the rope that acted as a sliding cradle. It looked simple—and crazy. I must have made some kind of exclamation, because, beside me, Roderick gave a little laugh.

"It's called abseiling. . . ." He himself was busy with a rope. "Quite a normal method of descent, and much the quickest. . . . No, Bill, I'll go. We'll shout up fast enough if we want reinforcements."

Rhodri had vanished. The boy Iain stayed by the spike of rock that anchored the rope, and Beagle was already on his way down. Nicholas turned back from the edge.

"I'm coming down," he said briefly.

Roderick, bending to anchor his own rope, shot him a swift upward look and hesitated. "You? I didn't know you climbed."

"No?" said Nicholas, not very pleasantly. Roderick's eyes flickered, but he merely said, mildly enough: "I'd better go first, perhaps."

And as quickly as Rhodri—and rather more smoothly —he was gone. Nicholas watched him down, with his back squarely turned to me where I sat huddled on my wet stone. Then, at a shout from below, he, too, laid hold of the ropes, and carefully lowered himself over the edge.

The little group of waiting men had moved forward to the brink of the gully, and once more there was about them, peering down into the echoing depths, that air of foreboding that gradually freezes through dread to certainty. I got up and moved to join them.

And almost at once a shout came from below—a wordless sound whose message was nevertheless hideously clear. I started forward, and felt Dougal Macrae's big hand close on my arm.

"Steady now!"

"He's found them!" I cried.

"Aye, I think so."

Major Persimmon was kneeling at the gully's edge; there were further exchanges of shouting, which the wind swept into nothingness. Then the group of men broke from its immobility into rapid and practiced activity, two more of the local rescue team preparing to descend, while the main party made off at some speed down the scree.

"Where are they going?"

"For the stretchers," said Dougal.

I suppose hope dies hard. My passionate hope, and my ignorance, between them, made me blind to his tone, and to the expressions of the other men. I pulled myself eagerly out of his grip, starting forward to the edge of the gully.

"Stretchers? They're alive? Can they possibly be still alive?"

Then I saw what was at the bottom of the gully. Beagle and Nicholas were carrying it between them, slowly making their awkward way across the slabs that funneled the rush of water. And there was no possible misapprehension about the burden that they were hauling from the fringes of the cascade. . . . I had forgotten that a dead body would be stiff, locked like some grotesque wood carving in the last pathetic posture of death. Navy trousers, blue jacket smeared and soaked almost to black, filthy yellow mittens on horror-splayed fingers . . . Marion Bradford. But it was no longer Marion Bradford; it was a hideous wooden doll that the men held between them, a doll whose head dangled loosely from a lolling neck. . . .

I went very quietly back to my stone, and sat down, staring at my feet.

Even when the stretchers came, I did not move. There was nothing I could do, but I somehow shrank from going back to the hotel now, alone—and Alma Corrigan showed no disposition to leave the place. So I stayed where I was, smoking too hard and looking away from the gully, along the grey flank of the mountain, while from behind me came the sounds of the rescue that was a rescue no longer. The creak and scrape of rope; a soft rush of Gaelic; grunts of effort; a call from Roderick, strained and distant; Beagle's voice, lifted in a sharp shout; Major Persimmon's, nearby, saying *"What? My God!"* then another splutter of Gaelic close beside me— this time so excited that I stirred uneasily and then looked round.

It was Dougal who had exclaimed. He and Major Persimmon were on their knees side by side, peering down into the gully. I heard Persimmon say again: *"My God!"* and then the two men got slowly to their feet, eyeing one another.

"He's right, Dougal."

Dougal said nothing. His face was like granite.

"What is it? What are they yelling about down there?" Alma Corrigan's voice rose sharply.

Bill Persimmon said: "She fell from the slab all right. The rope is still on her body. And it's been cut."

Her face was sallow under the bright scarf. "What— what d'you mean?"

He lifted a shoulder, and said wearily: "Just what I say. Someone cut the rope, and she fell."

Alma Corrigan said, in a dry little whisper: *"Murder . . . ."*

I said: "And Roberta Symes?"

His gaze flicked me absently as he turned back to the cliff's edge. "They haven't found her yet."

And they did not find her, though they searched that dreadful gully from end to end, and though for the rest of the day they toiled once more up and down the endless scree.

Chapter 11

THE SEARCH WENT ON ALL DAY. Towards late afternoon the wind dropped, only wakening from time to time in fitful gusts. The rain stopped, but great slate-colored clouds hung low, blotting out the Cuillin and crowding sullenly over the crest of Blaven. Marsco, away to the

north, was invisible, and a long way below us, Loch na
Creitheach lay dull and pewter-grey.

They finally got Marion Bradford's body down to the
mouth of the gully at about four o'clock. From high up
on the scree, I watched the somber little procession bump-
ing its difficult way over the wet heather, with the sad
clouds sagging overhead. It reached the lower spur of
An't Sròn and wound drearily along its crest, past the
pathetic irony of the celebration bonfire, and out of sight
over the end of the hill.

Dispiritedly I turned back to the grey scree, fishing for
another cigarette. The Coronation bonfire ... and tomorrow, in London, the bells would be ringing and the bands
playing, while here—there would be no celebration here,
tomorrow. The lonely bubbling call of the curlew, the
infinitely sad pipe of the golden plover, the distant drone
of the sea, these were the sounds that would hold Camasunary glen tomorrow, as they did now. And if Roberta
were still missing. . . .

I heard the scrape of boot on rock above me, and
looked up to see Roderick Grant edging his way down
one of the innumerable ledges that ran up to the cliff
above the Sputan Dhu. His head was bare, and the fair
hair was dark with the rain. He looked indescribably
weary and depressed, and one of his hands was bleeding.
I remembered what Marcia had told me, and wondered
suddenly if he had known of Marion Bradford's *penchant*
for him, and was feeling now some odd sort of self-
reproach.

His expression lightened a little when he saw me, then
the mask of strain dropped over it again. His eyes looked
slate-blue in the uncertain light.

"You should have gone back to the hotel," he said
abruptly. "You look done in."

"I suppose so," I said wearily. My hands were wet and
cold, and I was fumbling ineptly with matches. He took
me gently by the shoulders and pushed me down to a
seat on a boulder. I sat thankfully, while he flicked his
lighter into flame and lit my cigarette, then he pulled
open his haversack and produced a package.

"What have you had to eat?"

"Oh, sandwiches. I forget."

"Because it was far too long ago," said he. "Here—I

got a double chukker. Help me eat these. Did you have some coffee?"

"Yes."

He held out a flat silver flask. "Have a drop of this; it'll do the trick."

It did. It was neat Scotch, and it kicked me back to consciousness in five seconds flat. I sat up on my rock and took another sandwich.

He was eyeing me. "That's better. But all the same, I think you'd better go back to the hotel."

I shook my head. "I can't. Not yet. I'd never be able to settle down and wait, not now. We've got to find Roberta. Another night on the hill—"

His voice was gentle. "I doubt if another night will make much difference to Roberta, Janet."

"She *must* be alive," I said stubbornly. "If she'd fallen into the gully with Marion Bradford, she'd have been found. Dougal Macrae said she could have been stopped higher up, by a ledge or something. There must be places near the top of the gully—"

"I've raked the whole of the upper gully twice over," he said wearily. "Drury and I and Corrigan have been there all day. There's no sign of her."

"She must be somewhere." My voice sounded dogged and stupid. "She must have been hurt, or she'd have answered you; and if she was hurt, she can't have gone far. Unless—"

I felt my muscles tightening nervously as, perhaps for the first time, the possible significance of that severed rope end fully presented itself. I turned scared eyes to him.

"Roderick"—I used his name without thinking—"you were down in the gully. You saw Marion's climbing rope. That cut rope can only mean one thing, can't it?"

He dragged hard on his cigarette, and expelled a cloud of smoke like a great sigh. "Yes. Murder—again. . . ."

I said slowly: "And Dougal swears there *was* a third climber, but whether it was a man or woman he can't say."

He made a slight impatient gesture. "If he's to be believed."

"Oh, I think he is. If anyone in this world's dependable, I'd say it was Dougal Macrae. If there wasn't a third climber, then we've got to believe that it was Roberta who cut the rope, and that's fantastic."

"But is it?"

My eyes widened. "You can't believe that *Roberta*—"

"She was a beginner. If Marion fell, and was pulling her loose from her hold, she might panic, and—"

"I don't believe it! And what's more, neither do you!"

He gave a wry little smile. "No."

"So there *was* a third climber," I said, "and he cut the rope, so he's a murderer. He was there when Marion fell. And Roberta—whether she fell or not—can't be found. It doesn't add up to anything very pretty, does it?"

"You think *the murderer* removed Roberta?"

"What else can we think? We can't find her. If she was dead, he could safely have left her. If she was only injured, he'd have to silence her. He may have killed her and hidden her, hoping that the delay in finding the bodies would help him in some way or other." I fetched a sigh. "I don't know. I'm just in a dreary sort of whirl, praying she's all right and—oh God, yes, knowing all the time she can't be."

I got to my feet.

"Let's get on with this," I said.

The dark drew down, and all along the mountain slopes, indefatigably, the searchers toiled. Beagle and Rhodri MacDowell, who had been down with the stretcher, returned bringing food, soup, coffee, and torches from the hotel. We ate and drank, standing round in the gathering darkness. There was not much said: the men's faces were drawn and strained, their movements heavy. What little conversation there was related simply to accounts of areas searched and suggestions for further reconnaissance.

I found myself beside Ronald Beagle, who, despite the exacting role he had played in the rescue, was showing very little sign of strain. He was draining his mug of hot coffee as Alastair came up, seeming to loom over the smaller man in the darkness.

"That gully below the Sputan Dhu," he said abruptly. "What's the bottom like?"

Beagle glanced up at him. There was mild surprise in his voice. "Pretty rough. All devil's potholes and fallen boulders. The stream drops down a series of cascades to the foot of the scree. Why? I assure you we couldn't have missed her."

"Any caves or fissures in the sides of the gully?"

"Plenty." Ronald Beagle bent to put his coffee mug in the hotel's basket. "But there were four of us, and I assure you—"

"Can you assure me," said Alastair evenly, "that at least two of you searched each of these fissures?"

There was silence for a moment; I saw the rapid glow and fade, glow and fade, of Alastair's cigarette. Then another cigarette glowed beside it. Roderick's voice spoke from behind it.

"Why? What are you suggesting?"

"I'm suggesting that one of us here is a murderer," said Alastair brutally.

Hartley Corrigan's voice broke in. "That's a filthy thing to say! It's tantamount to accusing Beagle or Grant or Drury—"

"He's quite right, you know," said Beagle mildly. "It could quite easily be one of us. But why should it be in the murderer's interest to conceal the second body, once the first was found? It would certainly be to his interest to be the first to find her if she were still alive, so that he could silence her." He looked up at Alastair again. "But he didn't. I imagine every crevice in that gully was searched, solo and chorus, by every one of us."

"And that's a fact." Rhodri MacDowell spoke unexpectedly out of the darkness.

"Okay, okay," said Alastair. He looked at Beagle. "You know how it is. . . ."

"I know. It's quite all right."

The group was moving now, breaking and re-forming its knots of shadow-shapes, as men gathered once more into their parties for the search. I found Nicholas beside me.

He said shortly, his voice rough with fatigue: "This is absurd, Gianetta. Get back to the hotel at once."

I was too tired to resent his tone. "I can't give up yet," I said dully. "I couldn't stand sitting about waiting, listening with the Cowdray-Simpsons for the Everest news, and just wondering and wondering what was happening on the hill."

"There's no sense in your staying here," said Ronald Beagle. "You want to get back and rest, and find some way of taking your mind off this business. And talking of Everest—" He gave a jerk to his haversack, and raised his voice. I saw his teeth gleam in an unexpected grin.

"I forgot to tell you," he said to the dim groups scattered round him, "that the news came through on the A.F.N. a short while ago. They've done it. By God they have. They've climbed Everest."

There was a buzz of excitement, and for a moment the grim nature of the quest on which we were engaged was forgotten, as a host of eager questions was flung at him. He answered with his usual calm, but soon moved off, alone, and immediately afterwards the group broke up, and the parties vanished in various directions in the darkness to resume their search. I heard their voices as they moved away, animatedly discussing Beagle's announcement. He had, it seemed to me, deliberately kept back his news and then used it to galvanize the weary searchers into fresh activity. My respect for him increased.

Beside me, Nicholas spoke again, angrily: "Now look here, Gianetta—"

Roderick broke across it: "Leave her alone."

"What the hell do you mean?"

Torches were flashing nearby, and in their fitful flickering I could see Roderick's face. It was quite white, and blazing with a kind of nervous fury. His eyes were on Nicholas, and in that light they looked black and dangerous.

"What I said. What Janet does is nothing to do with you, and I rather fancy she prefers you to leave her alone."

It was a nasty, snarling little scene, and it had all blown up so quickly that I stood, gaping, between the pair of them, for a good fifteen seconds before I realized what was happening. This was Marcia's doing, blast her.

"Stop it, you two," I said sharply. "What I do is my own affair and nobody else's." I took hold of Roderick's arm, and gave it a little shake. "But he's right, Roderick. I'm no use here, and I'm going back now. So both of you leave me alone." I pulled my woolen gloves out of a pocket and began to drag them on over cold hands. "We're all tired and edgy, so for heaven's sake don't let's have a scene. I'm going to pack these thermos flasks and things, and take them straight down to the hotel, and then I'm going to bed."

I knelt down and began to pack mugs into the basket. I hadn't even glanced at Nicholas. He didn't say a word, but I saw him pitch his cigarette savagely down the hillside, then he turned in silence and plunged off into the darkness after Ronald Beagle. Above me, Roderick said hesitatingly:

"Have you got a torch?"

"Yes," I said. "Don't worry about me, I know my way. Go and help the others." I looked up then at him uncertainly. "And—Roderick."

"Yes?" His voice was still tight and grim.

"Find her, won't you?"

"I'll try." Then he, too, was gone. I packed all the debris I could find by the light of my torch, and then I sat down for a few minutes and lit another cigarette. I had just finished smoking one, but my nerves were still jumping, and the last little scene, with all its curious overtones, had upset me more than I wanted to admit.

It was quite dark now. Behind me the hill flashed with scattered torchlight, and I could hear, distorted by the gusts of wind, the occasional shouts of the searchers. In the intervals of the wind I heard the scrape of boots on rock, and, twice, away to my left, a sharp bark that I took to be the cry of a hill fox.

I got up at last, ground out my cigarette with my heel, lifted the basket, and began to pick my way down the mountainside. I gave the gully a very wide berth, and scrambled slowly and carefully, with the aid of my torch, down through the tumbled boulders of the scree. Halfway down, I knew, I would come upon the deer track that led, roughly but safely, to the lower spur of An't Sròn. Away below, a flock of oyster catchers flew up the glen from the shore, wrangling noisily among themselves. I could hear their cheery vulgar chirking echoing along the water of the loch, then falling silent. The wind blew strongly on my face, with its clear tang of sea and grass and peat. I let myself carefully down onto a muddy ledge and found that I was on the deer track.

Going was easier now, but I still went slowly and cautiously, hampered by basket and torch, which left me no hand free in case I slipped. It must have been well over an hour after I started my journey back, before I found myself, with relief, walking on the heather of the ridge that joined Blaven with An't Sròn.

I had been so afraid of stumbling, or of losing the deer track, that I had come down the hillside with my eyes glued to the little circle of ground that my torch lit at my feet. But as I reached the level heather of the ridge, I became conscious of a new element in the tangy wind that blew against my face. Even when I identified this as the smell of smoke, I still walked forward unalarmed, unrealizing.

Until I lifted my eyes and saw it, a pale climbing column of smoke, no more than a hundred yards ahead.

The bonfire. Someone had lit the bonfire. The smoke from the damp wood towered and billowed, ghostly against the black night, but there was a flickering glare at the heart of the smoke, and I heard the crackle as a flame leapt.

I suppose I stood there, looking at it, for a full half minute, while my slow brain registered the fact that somebody, who had not heard about the accident, had lit the celebration bonfire. Then another branch crackled, the smoke billowed up redly, and across in front of the glow moved the black figure of a man.

It was as if a shutter in my brain had clicked, and, in place of this, an older picture had flashed in front of me. A column of flame, with a man's shadow dancing grotesquely in front of it. A blackened pyre, with the body of a murdered girl lying across it like a careful sacrifice. . . .

Roberta!

It was for this that the murderer had kept Roberta.

I dropped the basket with a crash, and ran like a mad thing towards the smoking pyre. I don't know what I hoped to do. I was acting purely by instinct. I hurled myself forward, shouting as I ran, and I had the heavy torch gripped in my hand like a hammer.

There was an answering shout from the hill behind— close behind—but I hardly heeded it. I ran on, desperately, silent now but for my sobbing, tearing breath. The fire was taking hold. The smoke belched sideways in the wind, and whirled over me in a choking cloud.

I was there. The smoke swirled round me, billowing up into the black sky. The flames snaked up with the crack of little whips, and the crisscross of burning boughs stood out in front of them like bars.

I came to a slithering, choking halt at the very foot of the pyre, and tried to shield my eyes as I gazed upwards.

I saw the smoke fanning out under something that was laid across the top of the pile. I saw the glass of a wrist watch gleam red in the flame. I saw a boot dangling, the nails in the sole shining like points of fire.

I flung myself at the burning pile and clawed upwards at the arm and leg.

Then a shadow loomed behind me out of the smoke. A man's strong hands seized me and dragged me back. I whirled and struck out with the torch. He swore, and then he had me in a crippling grip. I struggled wildly, and I think I screamed. His grip crushed me. Then he tripped, and I was flung down into the wet heather, with my attacker's heavy body bearing me down.

Dimly, I heard shouting, the thud of feet, a voice saying hoarsely: *"Gianetta!"* Then someone dragged my assailant off me. I heard Alastair's voice say, in stupefaction: *Jamesy Farlane!* What goes on, in the name of God?" as he took the young man in a vicious grip. It was Dougal Macrae who hauled me onto my feet. I was shivering and, I think, crying. He said: "Are ye all right, mistress?"

I clung to him, and whispered through shaking lips: "On the fire—Roberta—*hurry.*"

He put an arm around me. His big body was trembling too, and as I realized why, my pity for him gave me the strength to pull myself together. I said, more calmly: "Is she dead?"

Another voice spoke. I looked up hazily. There was a man standing a little way from the bonfire. It was Hartley Corrigan, and he was looking down at the thing that lay at his feet.

His voice was without expression. He said: "It's not Roberta Symes. It's Beagle. And someone has cut his throat."

Chapter 12

I SLEPT LATE next morning, after a night of nightmares, and woke to a bright world. Mist still haunted the mountain tops, lying like snowdrifts in crevice and corrie, but the wind had dropped, and the sun was out. Blaven looked blue, and the sea sparkled.

But it was with no corresponding lift of the spirits that,

at length, I went downstairs, to be met by the news that
Roberta had not yet been found, and that the police had
arrived. I could not eat anything, but drank coffee and
stared out of the window of the empty dining room, until
Bill Persimmon, looking tired and grave, came and told
me that the police would like a word with me.

As luck would have it, the officer in charge of the
Macrae murder had come over from Elgol that morning,
to pursue some further inquiries relating to the earlier
case. So, hotter upon the heels of the new development
than any murderer could have expected, came the quiet-
eyed Inspector Mackenzie from Inverness, and with him
an enormous redheaded young sergeant called Hector
Munro. A doctor, hastily summoned in the small hours
by telephone, had already examined the bodies of Marion
and Beagle, and a constable had been dispatched to the
site of the new bonfire, to guard whatever clues might be
there for the Inspector to pick up, when he should have
finished his preliminary questions at the hotel.

This information was relayed to me hastily by Bill Persimmon, as he led me to a little sitting room beside the
residents' lounge, where the Inspector had his temporary
headquarters.

Absurdly enough, I was nervous, and was in no way
reassured when the Inspector turned out to be a kind-
looking middle-aged man with greying hair and deeply set
grey eyes, their corners crinkled as if he laughed a good
deal. He got up when I entered, and we shook hands
formally. I sat down in the chair he indicated, so that
we faced each other across a small table. At his elbow
the enormous redheaded sergeant, solemnly waiting with
a notebook, dwarfed the table, his own spindly chair, and,
indeed, the whole room.

"Well now, Miss Brooke...." The Inspector glanced
down at a pile of papers in front of him, as if he were
vague about my identity, and had to reassure himself.
"I understand that you only arrived here on Saturday
afternoon?"

"Yes, Inspector."

"And, before you came here, had you heard anything
about the murder of Heather Macrae?"

I was surprised, and showed it. "Why—no."

"Not even read about it in the papers?"

"Not that I recollect."

"Ah. . . ." He was still looking down at the table, talking casually. "And who told you about it?"

I said carefully, wondering what he was getting at: "I gathered, from hints that various people let drop, that something awful had happened, so I asked Mr. Grant about it, and he told me."

"That would be Mr. Roderick Grant?" He flicked over a couple of papers, and the sergeant made a note.

"Yes. And then Mr. Hay talked of it again next morning." I added politely, to the sergeant: "Mr. Hubert Hay. Footloose."

"Quite so." The Inspector's eyes crinkled momentarily at the corners. "Well, we'll let that go for the moment. I understand that it was you who found Mr. Beagle's body on the bonfire last night?"

"Yes. At least, I was first on the scene. I don't know who pulled him off the bonfire."

The Inspector looked straight at me for the first time, and I saw that his eyes were quite impersonal, remote, even, and very cold. The effect, in his homely pleasant face, was disconcerting and a little frightening. He said: "When was it that you first noticed that the fire had been lit?"

"Not until I was quite close to it. Do you know the hill, Inspector Mackenzie?"

"I've been on it a good bit in the past three weeks."

"Of course. How stupid of me."

He smiled suddenly. "And Hecky and I have a map. Now, Miss Brooke, just tell me in your own words what happened on your way down from the hill."

So I told him. He listened quietly, his grey eyes placidly inquiring. At his elbow the redheaded sergeant—equally placid—made notes in a competent shorthand.

". . . And then I saw a shadow, like a man, near the bonfire."

"Only one?"

"Yes."

"I take it that you didn't recognize him?"

"No."

"Was he carrying or hauling a body then?"

"Oh no. He was just moving about on the fringe of the smoke—it was billowing here and there, you know, in the wind. I remembered the—the other murder, and I thought it was Roberta being murdered this time—"

"Roberta?"

"Roberta Symes, the girl who's missing. Inspector, oughtn't we all to be out looking—?"

He said quietly: "There are men out now on the hill. Go on."

"That's all there is. I just ran towards the bonfire. I don't know what I imagined I could do. I saw there was something—a body—on top of it, and then just as I tried to get to the body before the fire did, the murderer attacked me."

"In actual fact," said the Inspector calmly, "it was Jamesy Farlane who attacked you."

I stared at him. "I know that. Surely—?"

He interrupted me. "Now. Let's get this picture right. You realize no doubt that Mr. Beagle cannot have been killed very long before you found him. You met or passed nobody at all on your way down to An't Sròn?"

"No one."

"Did you hear anything? Any footsteps, or—?"

"Nothing. I could hear the men shouting occasionally away above on the scree, but nothing else. When I saw the bonfire and screamed, someone shouted quite close behind me, but I hadn't heard him till then. The wind was strongish, you see, and—"

"Quite so." Once more he appeared to contemplate the table in front of him. "You last saw Mr. Beagle alive when the group broke up for the final search last night?"

"I—Are you allowed to ask leading questions, Inspector?"

He grinned. "I've already heard the answer to this one a dozen times. I'm saving time. Did you?"

"Yes."

"Did you see which way he went?"

"Downhill."

"Alone?"

"Yes."

"Sure?"

I regarded him levelly. "Quite."

"I see. Now let's get back to the bonfire, shall we? You ran towards it, and screamed. Did you recognize the shout that answered you—from close behind you, I think you said?"

"No, I didn't. But I assumed it was Alastair—Mr. Braine—because it was he who pulled Jamesy Farlane off me. He must have got there pretty quickly. Dougal Macrae was there too."

"Mr. Alastair Braine, then, was first on the scene—and very prompt." His voice was contemplative and pleasant. I felt my muscles tightening. "Who else was there?"

"Mr. Corrigan. He was standing by the bonfire. He—he must have pulled the body off." I swallowed, and added quickly: "He and Alastair probably came down together."

"No," said the Inspector gently to the table top. "Both gentlemen tell me they arrived independently." His grey eyes lifted to mine, suddenly hard and bright. "Who else was there?"

"Why—nobody."

"Jamesy Farlane and Dougal Macrae, Mr. Braine and Mr. Corrigan, all there within seconds of your scream. Who else?"

I looked at him. "That was all. I saw nobody else."

The grey eyes regarded me, then dropped. "Just so," said the Inspector vaguely, but I had the most uncomfortable impression of some conclusion reached in the last five minutes which was anything but vague. He shuffled a few papers in a desultory way, and said, without looking at me: "You booked your room a week ago?"

"I—yes."

"After the murder of Heather Macrae."

"I suppose so. I didn't know—"

"Quite. Sergeant Munro has your statement to that effect. . . . You booked your room, Miss Brooke, in the name of Drury, Mrs. Nicholas Drury."

It was absurd that he should be treating me as if I were a hostile witness, absurd that I should sit there with jumping nerves and tight-clasped hands just because his manner was no longer friendly.

I said, sounding both guilty and defiant: "That is my name."

"Then why did you change it to Brooke as soon as you got here? And why have you and your husband been at some pains to ignore one another's presence?"

"He's—not my husband." I found myself hurrying to explain. "We were divorced four years ago. I didn't know he was here. When I saw him the first evening I was horribly embarrassed, and I changed to my maiden name to avoid questions."

"I—see." Then, suddenly, he smiled. "I'm sorry if I've distressed you, Miss Brooke. And you've been very helpful—very helpful indeed."

But this, oddly enough, was far from reassuring me. I said sharply: "But why does all this matter? Surely it's all settled? You've got the murderer, and—"

His brows shot up. "Got the murderer?"

"Jamesy Farlane!" I cried. "Jamesy Farlane! Who else could it be? He was at the bonfire, and he attacked me there. What more do you want?"

"A bit more," said Inspector Mackenzie, with a little smile. "Farlane's story is that he was going back from the hotel after bringing the stretcher in. He was at the foot of An't Sròn when he saw the bonfire go up. He went up the hill as fast as he could, and was nearly at the top when he heard you scream, and then you came running and, he says, flung yourself at the bonfire. He thought you were going to be burned, and he jumped in and hauled you off. You hit at him, and in the ensuing struggle you both fell down the heather slope. ... Is that right, Hecky?"

"That's right, sir." Hector Munro nodded his red head.

"You see?" said Inspector Mackenzie to me.

"It might even be true," I said.

He grinned. "So it might. Especially as Dougal Macrae was with him at the time."

There was a sharp little silence. Then he rose and began to gather up his papers. I stood up.

"If I may," he said, "I'll see you again later, but just at present I'd better get up onto An't Sròn." He held the door for me with punctilious courtesy. "You'll be about all day, I take it?"

"I'll be up on the hill myself," I said, and was unable to keep the asperity out of my voice. "There's still somebody missing, you know."

"I hadn't forgotten," he said gravely, and shut the door behind me.

Chapter 13

TWO NIGHTS AND A DAY—it was a very long time to be out on the mountainside. It think that, by now, we had all given up all prospect of finding Roberta alive. I had, to begin with, built a lot of hope upon the fact that there had been no trace of her within range of Marion Bradford's dead body. A direct fall in the same place must have killed her. The fact that she was nowhere near appeared to indicate some not-too-serious injury which had allowed her to crawl away into shelter. But, of course, if she were still conscious, she must have heard the search parties. And two nights and a day, even in summer weather, was a very long time. . . .

I had by now abandoned my grisly theory that the murderer—the third climber—had taken Roberta away, alive or dead, for reasons of his own. If the murderer of the bonfires and the murderer of the cut climbing rope were one and the same—which was so probable as to be a certainty—then, surely he would hardly have killed poor Beagle for his second bonfire if he had had Roberta's body handy.

That he had any real motive for killing Ronald Beagle I could not believe. It seemed more than ever certain that we were dealing with a maniac. There was a causeless crazy flavor about the killings that was nauseating. Hubert Hay's word "sacrifice" occurred to me again, with shuddering force.

But where these two apparently ritual killings fitted with the deaths of Marion and Roberta I had no idea. At least, I thought, trudging once again up the deer track behind Hubert Hay, there was something we could *do*. The finding of Roberta, or Roberta's body, might help the police a little in their hunt for what was patently a madman.

The sun was still brilliant in the blue heaven. Yesterday, under the heavy grey sky, it had been easy to see the mountainside as the background to tragedy, but today, with the sunlight tracing its gold-foil arabesques on the young bracken, and drawing the hot coconut smell from the gorse, Blaven was no longer the sinister mountain that it had been yesterday. It was alive with the summer. The mountain linnets were playing over scrubs of bright furze, chirping and trilling, and everywhere in the corners of the grey rock glowed the vivid rose-purple of the early bell heather.

The search parties seemed at last to have abandoned the Black Spout, and were scattered about the mountain, still searching the screes and slopes of deep heather. One of the parties, Hubert Hay told me, had climbed higher up the cliffs above the Sputan Dhu, and was out of sight in the upper reaches of the mountain. I realized, as I scanned once again the acre upon acre of steep rocky scree, split by its gullies and fissures, how people could lie for a week, a month, out in the mountains, and their bodies not be found. And there were still, Hubert Hay told me, climbers lost years ago, of whom no trace had yet come to light.

As we reached the point where, yesterday, I had met Roderick climbing down from the Black Spout, we heard a shout, and saw, away to our right, a small party of men, one of whom—it looked like Hartley Corrigan—waved his arm and called something.

"Do you suppose they've found her?" I asked breathlessly.

"It doesn't look like it," returned Hubert Hay. "They may have decided on some new plan of search. I'll go along and have a word with them."

He began to make his way towards the other party, and I, left alone, stood for a while gazing up at the rocks above me. I was, I noticed, almost directly below the spot where Heather Macrae had been found. For a moment I dallied with the macabre fancy that there, upon that blackened ledge, we would find Roberta lying. Then I shook the thought away like the rags of last night's bad dream, and turned my eyes instead to the more accessible route which led towards the climb over the Black Spout.

I knew that the area had been searched already; searched, moreover, by a team of men who knew far more about the hill than I. But there is something in all of us which refuses to be satisfied with another report, however reliable, that someone else has looked for something and failed to find it. We cannot rest until we have looked for ourselves. And it was surely possible, I told myself, that some corner or hole or crevice of this awful country might have been overlooked.

I began doggedly to scramble up towards the tumble of rocks and heather at the side of the Sputan Dhu.

It was terrible going. The rock was dry today, and there was no wind, but each boulder represented a major scramble, and between the rocks were treacherous holes, thinly hidden by sedge and heather. I was soon sweating freely, and my head was swimming from too much peering under slabs and down the chutes of small scree that tunneled below the larger rocks. I struggled on, without realizing how high I had climbed, until exhaustion made me pause and straighten up to look back down the way I had come.

And almost at once something caught my eye—a tiny point of light among the heather, a sparkle as of an infinitesimal amber star. I saw the gleam of metal, and stooped to look more closely.

It was a broach of a kind very common in souvenir shops in Scotland, a circle of silvery metal set with a cairngorm. I stooped for it, suddenly excited. Roberta— surely Roberta had been wearing this on that first evening at the hotel? I wiped the dirt off it, then lit a cigarette and sat down with the brooch in my hand, considering it. It meant no more, of course, than that Roberta had been this way—and that I already knew from Dougal Macrae's testimony. But for me that winking amber star had somehow the excitement of discovery about it that set me scanning the empty slopes about me with renewed hope.

I was out of sight of the party, and could no longer hear their voices. The only sounds that held the summer air were the rush of the waterfall and the sudden rich burst of song from an ouzel I had disturbed from his perch. I frowned up at the steep pitch of rock above the gully, trying to picture what might have happened there two days ago.

Looking back now, I can realize that this was perhaps one of the queerest moments in the whole affair. If I had not been so abysmally ignorant—and so stupid—over the business of that climb across the Sputan Dhu, if I had worked on the evidence plainly available (as the others were even now working), I, too, would have abandoned the gully and searched elsewhere, and the story would have had a very different ending. But I sat there in the sun, smoking and piecing together my own bits of evidence, and deciding that, come what may, I had to finish seeing for myself if Roberta was on this side of the Sputan Dhu. So I stubbed out my cigarette and got up to resume my search.

I have no idea how long I took. I clambered and slithered and peered, pushing aside mats of heather and wood rush, and crawling into the most unlikely places. At first I called occasionally, my breathless *"Roberta!"* ringing queerly back from the cliffs above. Soon I was too exhausted to call but climbed and searched in a grim, hard-breathing silence, brought, minute by minute, to acknowledge that Roderick had been right when he said that he had searched every inch of the place. Roberta was not there.

At length, when I was all but giving up, my foot slipped when I was investigating a ledge. This was wide enough, and I suppose I was in no actual danger, but the brink of the ledge overhung the gully itself, and I was so badly frightened that I had to sit down, my back pressed against the wall of the rock, to collect my wits and my courage.

The sun poured down, slashing the rock with purple shadows. The towering cliffs shut out all sound but the rush of the lonely water. I might have been hundreds of miles from anywhere. The stillness was thick, frightening, uncanny. I sat still, listening to my own heartbeats.

It was then that I heard the moan.

From somewhere to my left it came, to the left and behind me.

I was on my feet in a flash, fatigue and fright alike forgotten.

"Roberta!" My voice was shrill and breathless. I waited.

It came again, a tiny animal whimpering. It seemed to come from somewhere along the ledge, somewhere back from it, inside the very rock. . . . I turned my back resolutely to the gully and my face to the cliff, and went as quickly as I dared towards the sound.

I came to a jutting rock, a corner, and peered round it, with my heart thudding in my throat. Beyond the buttress the ledge ran along the gully side, rising gradually and dwindling to a mere crack in the cliff. I could see the whole of it from where I stood. There was nothing there. Nothing.

I called again: "Roberta!"

I waited. There was no sound. The sun beat upon the empty rock.

"Roberta!"

There it was again, the tiny moaning.

I squeezed cautiously past the corner, and along the ledge. This was wide enough at first even for me, who am not used to mountains, but when I found it growing narrower, and taking a nasty outward slant at the same time, I stopped, bewildered and, once more, afraid. There was certainly nothing on the ledge. And, just as certainly, this ledge had already been reached. I had seen the imprint of boots which led as far as the corner. I was imagining things.

In that moment I heard the little whimper of pain again, but this time back to my left.

I looked back the way I had come, almost giddy now with bewilderment and excitement, my heart thudding, and my legs and wrists none too steady.

Then I saw the answer to the riddle. I had pressed past the jutting buttress of rock at the corner, without seeing that behind it, and running sharply back into the face of the cliff, was a narrow fissure. Most of the opening was masked by a hanging mat of weeds and heather, but there was a little space below this, through which someone might have crawled. . . .

I tore at the heather mat with desperate hands. It was tough, but chunks of it came away, and I flung it down the gully. Pebbles and peat spattered down onto the ledge. I yanked at a great trail of green and threw it down, so that the sunlight streamed past me into what was, in effect, a small dry cave.

She was there, all right. She was lying in a little curled huddle, her back against the wall of the cave. One leg stuck out at an ugly angle, and her hands were torn and covered with dirt and dried blood.

But she was alive. I flew across the cave to kneel beside her. Her eyes were shut, and the bright face that I remembered was a frightening grey-white, with a film of sweat over it like cellophane. The flesh was pulled back from the bones, so that her nose jutted out as sharp as a snipe's beak.

I thrust a shaking hand inside the brave red jacket and tried to find her heart. . . .

A man's shadow fell across the floor of the cave.

Chapter 14

RODERICK'S VOICE SAID: "My God, you've found her!"

I turned with a great sob of relief. "Oh, Roderick—oh, thank heaven someone's come! She's alive, and—"

"*Alive?*" His voice was incredulous. He took a stride across the cave, towering over us both. "*Alive?*"

"Yes. Yes, she is! I heard her moaning—that's how I found her."

He was down on his knees beside me now, his hands moving over Roberta. His face was grim.

"Yes, she's alive, but only just, Janet. I'm very much afraid—" He broke off, while his hands gently explored her head. She whimpered and moved a little. I said: "I'll stay with her, Roderick. You go and get the others. You'll go faster than me!"

He hardly seemed to hear me; he was still intent on Roberta. He looked remote, absorbed. When he spoke, it was with suddenly impersonal authority. "Janet, I left my haversack at the end of the ledge. You'll find my brandy flask in the pocket. Get it, will you?"

I went quickly. The sunshine met me in a dazzle of light and warmth as I stepped through the cave door. Behind me Roberta whimpered again, and said something in the blurred little voice of delirium. I caught the word *"Marion. . . ."*

It halted me in mid-stride, as the implications—the terrifying implications—of our discovery of Roberta came fully to me for the first time. I swung round. Roderick turned his head, and my frightened eyes met his. And beneath their still impersonal coolness I saw the same thought that was driving my heart in sickening jerks against my ribs.

"Roderick. . . ." I almost whispered it. "Roderick, she—she knows who did it."

There was grim twist to his mouth. "I realize that," he said. "And by God she's going to stay alive till she tells us. Get that brandy, please."

"We ought to wrap her up first. Have my coat. . . .We've got to get her warm somehow until we can call the others." I began to take off my coat. He followed suit rapidly, and I knelt down to wrap the now quiescent Roberta as warmly as I could in the two garments.

He added, still with that grim note to his voice: "And I'm not going for help either, to leave you here with this amount of potential dynamite; nor are you going to wander this hill alone any more, my dear. You fetch that brandy while I have a look at her leg, and then you'd better get along above the end of the ledge and just yell bloody murder till somebody comes. And if you don't like the look of whoever comes just yell bloody murder for me." He smiled suddenly. "And I'll be there. Now hurry."

"All right," I said. But as I tucked Roberta's cold hands gently inside my coat and made to rise, she began to stir once more, restlessly. The grey lips parted again in a whimper, and I saw that her eyelids were flickering.

"She's coming to," I whispered. My heart began to thump violently. Roderick's hand gripped my shoulder.

Then Roberta's eyes opened wide; they were dark and filled with pain, but sensible. For a moment she stared at me, as if bewildered, then her gaze moved beyond me.

Someone else was coming along the ledge.

Roberta's hands moved feebly under mine, like frightened animals. Her eyes dilated in an unmistakable look of pure terror. Then she fainted again.

I looked around. Framed in the narrow doorway of the cave was Hartley Corrigan, with Nicholas just behind him. And I could hear Alastair's voice as he followed the others along the ledge.

Alma Corrigan was waiting at the end of the ledge, and was now summoned with a shout. With the coming of the others my responsibility had lightened, and I had time to feel the slackening of nervous tension that comes with reaction. All at once exhaustion seemed to sweep over me like a drowning wave, and it was with feelings of unmixed thankfulness that I found myself elbowed aside by Mrs. Corrigan as she proceeded, with Roderick, to take charge of Roberta. I heard her giving rapid orders for first aid, while Roderick curtly deputed Nicholas to go and summon the other searchers and commandeer a stretcher.

The cave was now uncommonly crowded, but, remembering that look of terror in Roberta's eyes, I stayed where I was. I did go out onto the ledge, but there I remained, leaning against the rock in the sunlight, watching the others inside. If any of those people was the murderer who had sent Roberta to her death, it hardly seemed likely that he could finish his work here and now before she could speak and identify him—but I was taking no risks. I leaned there against the warm rock, and watched the others in the cave ministering to Roberta.

Presently I heard a shout from Nicholas, away up near the main cliff. This was answered by a more distant call. And after that, it did not seem so very long before the stretcher party arrived, and I could at last abandon my post and leave the ledge to them.

Dougal Macrae was with them, and the boy Iain, and Hubert Hay, who was certainly not the third climber, since he had been with me on Sgurr na Stri when Marion fell to her death. Roberta would be safe enough now—that is, if the murderer's work had not been already done too well, and she were to die of exposure.

But at least she had been found. The long strain was over. I sat among the heather, waiting for the stretcher to be brought off the ledge, and lifted my face to the sun, shutting my eyes and feeling, for the first time for two days, a sense of relaxation. The warm, sweet heather-smelling afternoon insisted, with every lark note, every linnet call, on the normality of the day and place. Even when, with mutterings, and cautious scrapings of boot on stone, the the stretcher was maneuvered along the ledge and balanced onto the scree, even then I still felt strangely lighthearted, as though the worst were over.

I had forgotten that Roberta had only to open her mouth and speak, and that a man—a man I knew—would hang by the neck until he was dead and then be buried in quicklime in a prison yard.

Inspector Mackenzie, with the enormous Hecky and Neill, the young local constable, was on An't Sròn when the stretcher was brought down. Hecky stayed where he was, and continued what was apparently a minute examination of the ground round the bonfire, but Inspector Mackenzie, after one glance at Roberta, summoned young Neill from his job, and with him accompanied the stretcher back to the hotel.

As soon as he was told that I had found Roberta, he dropped back from the main party with me, and began to question me. I told him, as exactly as I could, what had passed. He listened quietly, and as soon as I had finished, he took me through it all again, putting a question here and there, until I must have repeated every action and every word from the moment I heard the first moan, to the arrival of the stretcher party. As I told my story, trudging wearily beside him down the valley, I found that the precarious tranquillity that had lit my little hour upon the hillside had already vanished, a snow-on-the-desert passing that left me picking my old lonely way through the grey wastes of uncertainty and desolation. And that little cold wind of terror fumbled and plucked again, ice-fingered, at my sleeve, so that I stumbled once or twice in my narrative. But I recounted, honestly and flatly enough, all that I remembered, and left him to draw what conclusions he would.

Then he surprised me. He looked sideways at me and said abruptly: "I'm putting young Neill on to guard yon lassie, and we'll send for a nurse straightaway. But we'll not get one before tomorrow at soonest, as the doctor told me this morning that the district nurse is tied up just now with a tricky case. So someone's got to look after Miss Symes till a nurse comes. Do you know anything about nursing?"

"A little, I suppose, but—"

"That's fine. Will you do it? Stay with her tonight and watch her for me?"

"Why, of course," I said. "But surely someone else—I mean isn't there anyone more competent, more practiced, perhaps, than I am? Mrs. Corrigan seems to know her stuff, and I imagine Mrs. Persimmon—"

"No doubt," he said drily. "But has it not struck you, ma'am, that you're the only woman in the hotel who wasn't here at the time of the first murder?"

"I—I suppose I am. But, Inspector, you can't suspect a *woman*, surely? I mean—"

"Maybe not," he said, "but Mrs. Corrigan and Mrs. Persimmon have husbands. And I want *no one* in that room who might be in any way—er—involved." He shot me a queer look. "No one, on any excuse whatever. You follow me?"

"If you mean Nicholas," I said tartly, "I'm hardly 'involved' with him, and I assure you he's not likely to be admitted."

His mouth relaxed a little. "Now, now, lassie," he said, almost indulgently, "I wasn't meaning any such thing. Then I take it you'll do it?"

"Of course." I looked at him curiously. "Do you mean to tell me that I'm the only person here you don't suspect?"

"Let's say," he said cautiously, "that I don't suspect you of wanting to kill Roberta Symes."

And with that, we reached the hotel. Since Marion Bradford's body was in the room which she had shared with Roberta, and this had been locked by the police, I suggested that Roberta should be given the other bed in my room. The offer was approved by the Inspector, and accepted gratefully by the Persimmons, who were already harassed beyond belief. I left her being tucked up by Mrs. Persimmon and Mrs. Cowdray-Simpson, with Neill and the Inspector in attendance, and went along to have a bath.

When eventually I got back to my room I found that a bright fire had been kindled on the hearth, and that a kettle was already singing on the bars. All the apparatus for making hot drinks was there, and a half bottle of brandy gleamed on the bedside table.

The Inspector had gone, but Mrs. Persimmon was still busy over something by the hearth, and Neill rose from the chair by the fire and grinned shyly at me. He was a tall, overgrown lad of perhaps twenty, with graceful coltish movements, and the black hair and blue eyes of the true Celt. He said: "The doctor will be here soon, Mistress Brooke. Inspector Mackenzie told me to tell you. He says will you stay here with me till then?"

"Of course. Do we do anything for her meanwhile?"

Mrs. Persimmon rose to her feet. "We've packed her in hot-water bottles," she said. "She's as warm as we can get her, so all we can do now is wait for the doctor." She bent in a harassed way over Roberta's bed, twitching the blankets unnecessarily into place. She was a small woman, with a round face that normally was good-humored, and wispy, untidy brown hair. Her eyes were of the true glass-grey that you so seldom see, clear and lovely, but just now they were puckered and clouded with worry. "If she comes round enough to swallow, you could give her a little sweet tea—and I'll go down now and make some really good clear broth. But that's all we can do for the moment."

"Except," said Neill softly, "to watch her."

We both looked at him. I said uncertainly: "It all sounds very—very frightening, Neill. Does he really expect the murderer to try and get her in here?"

He spread out calloused, beautifully shaped hands. "If she talks, we can hang him," he said simply.

I went over to the bed and looked at her. She was lying very quietly now, and though I fancied that her skin had lost some of its icy glaze, it still had a tight-stretched pallor that was frightening. Her face was pinched and small; her body, too, was still and small in its packed blankets. Not dangerous; not "potential dynamite"; not worth the ghastly risk of silencing her. . . . It seemed impossible that those dry lips should ever speak again.

But even as I turned from the bedside she stirred and moaned and her eyelids fluttered. The dark head shifted restlessly on the pillow.

"Here," said Mrs. Persimmon from the hearth. "Here's the tea."

With anxious concentration we fed a few drops of the weak sweet stuff between her lips, and saw with delight the faint ripple of the throat muscles as she swallowed. I began, spoonful by spoonful, to pour the life-giving glucose into her, watching anxiously for any sign of change in that effigy of a face.

"I'll go and see about the broth," said Mrs. Persimmon at length, and went out.

The telephone rang. I jumped violently, spilling tea on the bedclothes. Neill lifted the receiver, listened and then said to me: "The Inspector's on his way up, ma'am. The doctor's here."

"Thank heaven for that!" I said fervently.

"Yes indeed."

A minute later we admitted Inspector Mackenzie and the doctor, and thankfully watched the competent way in which the latter examined Roberta. At length he pulled the bedclothes back over her, and looked across the bed at the Inspector.

"I can't find anything wrong except the leg," he said brusquely. "Bruises and lacerations, yes; they'll heal, given time. But we'll have to deal with the leg now. I'll need Mary Persimmon to help me, and someone else."

He glanced at me from under inquiring brows, but the Inspector intervened. "No, Miss Brooke's done enough for today, and besides, she has to be night nurse. Tell Mrs. Persimmon to bring one of the maids up with her, and I'll stay here myself. There's a telephone, doctor, if you want to give your orders."

"What? Oh, ah, yes." The doctor lifted the receiver, and began to dictate a list of his requirements.

Inspector Mackenzie turned to me. "I've asked the cook to give you something to eat as soon as possible," he said. "It'll be ready in the kitchen in ten minutes or so. You go on down, lassie. I'll call you when we want you back."

I gave another look at the small figure in the bed, and then made my way downstairs to the lounge.

Chapter 15

RODERICK WAS IN THE HALL. He must have been waiting for me, because, as soon as I appeared, he strode towards the foot of the stairs, looking anxious.

"Is she all right? What does the doctor say?"

"He didn't say very much," I replied. "He's found no actual damage beyond the broken leg, but I imagine it's the two nights in the cave that will kill her if anything does."

"What does he think of her chances?"

"He didn't say. I suppose she has as good a chance as anyone could have after what she's been through. She's young and very strong, and she did find herself a dry corner out of the wind and rain."

"She's still unconscious, of course?"

"Oh yes."

"She'll pull through it," he said confidently. "Once they get the leg set—I suppose they're doing that now?"

"Yes. Mrs. Persimmon's helping. They sent me down, I'm glad to say."

"And I'm glad they did. You look washed out, Janet."

I smiled. "Thank you for nothing."

"Sorry, but it's true." He was still looking worried. "You won't have to go back and sit with her, will you?"

"I think the Inspector wants me to stay in the room tonight."

"But that's absurd!" he said angrily. "You've done more than enough for one day! Why can't Mrs. Corrigan stay with her?"

"She's done quite as much as I have."

"Well, Mrs. Cowdray-Simpson, then?"

I said, carefully: "Inspector Mackenzie has allowed me to understand that he doesn't include me in his list of suspects."

"He doesn't—?" He broke off, and his blue eyes narrowed. "Surely he doesn't suspect *any* of the women?"

"I rather think he suspects everybody," I said, uncomfortably. "At any rate, I'm not married to a suspect either, you see."

He opened his mouth as if to speak, and then shut it again in a hard line. His eyes slid away from mine and he studied the pattern of the carpet.

I swallowed, and said hastily: "I'll be all right, Roderick. All I have to do is give her a drink every now and again, and I can get some sleep between times. In fact it's terribly snug in there, with a fire, and a kettle to make tea, and all the works!"

"Does the Inspector——" He paused, and shot a quick glance round the hall, then lowered his voice. "Does the Inspector think there's still any danger to Roberta from—him?"

The last syllable fell queerly, whispered in the empty hall. I found myself lowering my voice in reply.

"I think so. But he's taking precautions. Roberta'll be safe enough, and, by the same token, so will I." I smiled at him again. "So don't worry!"

"Very well, then, I won't. As a matter of fact"—his voice was suddenly grave, and a little abstracted—"as a matter of fact, I think you're probably the only person in the hotel who isn't—"

"Suspected of murder?"

"No. Who isn't in danger from the murderer."

He looked at me then, with a strange hesitant look that seemed to be mingled of both pity and dread, and something else that I found it hard to read. I felt my heart jump and twist painfully inside my ribs, and I could not meet his look. I turned sharply away towards the lounge door, saying in a tight, flat little voice: "I'll go and ring for a drink."

There seemed to be a crowd of people in the lounge, all gathered into small groups near the blazing fire. The air was a hiss of whispered conversations, which ceased abruptly as I came in. Heads swiveled, eyes stared, and then a fusillade of questions met me.

"How is she?" came simultaneously from Mrs. Cowdray-Simpson, her husband, Hubert Hay, and Alastair. Alma Corrigan's quick *"Has she said anything yet?"* cut across it like a knife.

I crossed to the fire and held my hands to the blaze. "The doctor's with her now, setting her leg. Apart from that, the damage appears to be superficial, and the doctor said nothing to me about her chances of recovery from the exposure." I looked at Alma Corrigan, who was twisting an empty whisky glass round and round in her fingers.

She looked, I thought, frightened. I said: "I don't think she's said anything yet."

As I turned to ring for a drink, I saw that Hartley Corrigan had moved up near his wife, and had sat down on the arm of her chair. It made a nice change, anyway, I thought, and wondered, a trifle sardonically, where Marcia was at this moment. One thing was certain, she was well out of whatever was going on here, though just now I would have welcomed the company of one other person in the same equivocal position as myself. There was nothing overt in the manner of anyone in the room to suggest that they knew or resented the fact that I alone was free from police suspicion, but still I felt isolated among them, uncomfortably a sheep in the middle of the goats. And there had been something oddly protective about that gesture of Hartley Corrigan's.

Mrs. Cowdray-Simpson looked up again from the inevitable knitting. "I presume—I hope—the police will take adequate precautions to protect that girl from this beast that's loose among us?"

The phrase sounded curiously shocking, and the speaker seemed to realize this, for the pale eyes behind her spectacles moved round the group, and she said, almost defensively: "There's a murderer in the room. You can't get away from that fact."

"Not necessarily," said Alastair, rather drily. "We're not all here. Grant, Drury, Persimmon, not to mention Jamesy Farlane . . . they lengthen the odds a little, Mrs. Crowdray-Simpson." He gave a hard little laugh that held no trace of amusement.

"What odds do I lengthen a little?" This was from Roderick, pushing through the swinging doors with a glass in either hand.

"We're just beginning to take seriously the fact that someone in this hotel is a murderer," said Alastair.

Roderick gave me a glass, and his eyes met mine in a quick look. He said, a little coldly: "Is anything to be gained by discussing it here? I imagine the police have it pretty well in hand. They can usually be trusted to do their own job."

"If they only look after that girl Roberta, and pull her round," said Mrs. Cowdray-Simpson, "she'll do the job for them."

"There'll be a constable watching her all night," I said.

"Young Neill Graham? Is that quite—adequate?"

I hesitated, and then said: "I'm staying with her too." I added, lamely: "She's in my room."

"Oh. . . ." Once again I felt the imperceptible withdrawal of the group, leaving me, as it were, marooned alone on the hearthrug, isolated by my innocence.

"Won't you be frightened?" This from Alma Corrigan. Was there, or was I imagining it, a trace of malice in her tone?

"I don't think so." I took a drink, and gave the group a quick look over the rim of my glass. "Where's Mr. Drury?"

"I think he went out to the garage." It was Hubert Hay who answered. "He's lost a book, and he thinks he left it in his car."

"Why?" asked Alma Corrigan, and this time I certainly heard the venom in her voice. "Has the Inspector asked for a report on our movements?"

I felt myself go scarlet, but I held onto my temper, and said, very evenly: "I am not, as you imply, Mrs. Corrigan, appointed by the police to spy on you all. I happen to be in the lucky position of not being a suspect, simply because I wasn't here when the first murder was committed, and since the odds are that we only have one murderer and not two, I can't be guilty. So the Inspector can leave me with Roberta until the nurse comes."

"It's monstrous to suggest—" began Roderick, hotly, to Alma Corrigan, but I cut across him.

"It's all right, Roderick. And the suggestion isn't so very monstrous after all. I'm certainly co-operating with the police—I hope we all are. And if that includes giving the Inspector an account of anyone's movements at any time, I'll do my utmost to describe them for him."

"Well!" said Alma Corrigan. "I must say—" Her husband dropped a hand on her arm, and she broke off. I said to her, coldly: "I should hardly need to point out that this isn't a case of the police *versus* a bunch of suspects. It's a case of the murderer *versus* every single other person here."

"Good for you!" said Hubert Hay unexpectedly.

Colonel Cowdray-Simpson cleared his throat. His face looked all at once remote and austere, with a curious withdrawn intelligence that his gentleness had hidden before. It was a look both forbidding and compassionate, the look of a judge rather than of a soldier. I found myself wondering if he were a magistrate. "It is more than that, my dear young lady," he said to me. "Each case of murder is a case of the murderer *versus* every civilized human being. Once a man has put his hand to murder he is automatically outcast. I would go further than that. I would assert that once the very idea of extreme physical violence has occurred to a man as an acceptable solution to any problem, then he is in danger of forfeiting his claim to consideration as a civilized being."

"That's a strong statement, sir," said Roderick.

"I happen to feel strongly about it," retorted the Colonel.

"Do you apply the same principle to nations as to individuals? You, a military man?"

"I do."

"To acts of war?"

"To acts of aggression. It seems to me a denial of the intellectual progress of centuries, for a nation to consider violence as a tool of policy."

"All the same," said Alma Corrigan mulishly, "it's absurd that we should all be treated as suspects. The police *must* have some idea who did it."

"If they haven't now," said Hubert Hay, "they certainly will have as soon as Roberta Symes opens her mouth."

There was a nasty little silence.

I set down my glass with a *click* on the glass-topped table. "Well," I said, "for the sake of everybody here who isn't a murderer, I promise you that Roberta will be kept safe until she *does* open her mouth."

Then I walked out of the room.

It didn't take much, I thought, to skin the veneer of politeness and sophistication off people who were in some kind of danger. There had been some strong undercurrents there in the lounge tonight, and I had a feeling that, if one had been able to trace them out, one would be a fair way to solving the mystery. On the face of it, I thought (as I crossed the hall and started down the dark passage towards the kitchen and back premises), I would be inclined to absolve the Colonel. He had delivered himself so convincingly of his principles; but then (I added a despairing rider), that, surely, might be just what a murderer would do? And, heaven knew, our murderer was clever. He was an actor who could hide the instincts of a werewolf under an impeccably civilized exterior. Nobody in the lounge tonight, hearing his own condemnation, the statement of his utter isolation from the rest of us, had so much as batted an eyelid. But then, of course, the murderer might not have been in the lounge. . . . There were other possibilities, as Alastair had pointed out.

I turned a corner of the passage and ran straight into Nicholas.

Literally ran into him, I mean. He caught me by the arms and steadied me, peering down in the dimness of the passage.

"Why," he said softly, "it's our little copper's nark. The Inspector's not down this way, darling."

I did lose my temper then. I blazed at him, pulling against the pressure of his hands. "Let me go, damn you! *Let me go!* Don't you dare to speak to me like that! You've no right—"

"So you keep telling me. Where are you going?"

"That's none of your damned business!"

"It's anybody's business in this murderous locality to stop you from wandering about in the dark alone."

"I'm going to the kitchen to get some food," I said waspishly, "and I'm in a hurry."

He did not move. "Where's the boy friend?"

"What d'you mean?"

"Your *preux chevalier* with the golden hair. Why isn't he playing bodyguard?"

"You always did have a filthy tongue, Nicholas," I said bitterly.

"I did, didn't I?" He grinned sardonically. "You could say it's a valuable stock in trade as a writer, though perhaps as a husband—"

"Exactly. Now let me go."

"Just a moment. I'm quite serious, as it happens, Gianetta. It seems to me you're altogether too fond of wandering about the place alone—or with somebody you don't know. If you had a grain of sense you'd know this chap meant business. Aren't you scared?"

"I wasn't," I said tartly, "until three minutes ago."

I don't know what made me say it. The instant the words were out I regretted them, but it was too late. He dropped his hands from my arms and stood looking down at me in the semidarkness. I thought he must hear the thudding of my heart.

"O-ho . . ." he said at length, and then, very softly: "Sits the wind in that quarter?"

I was silent. I wanted to run from him, towards the lights and warmth of the kitchen, but I was held there, nailed to the passage wall by the hammer blows of my own heart.

Nicholas said: "So you're afraid I'll kill you, Gianetta *mia*? . . . Do you really think I'd do that, Gianetta? Cut that pretty throat, Gianetta . . . and all for what? Auld lang syne?"

"Do you need a reason?" My voice was a whisper that sounded strange to me. This could not be happening; this fantastic conversation could not be taking place. . . . "Do you need a reason?" I whispered.

He did not reply. He stood looking at me in silence, his face, in that uncertain light, quite inscrutable. At length he said, in quite a different tone: "What's your proof?"

I almost jumped. "I haven't any."

"If you had, would you hand me over—for auld lang syne?"

Fantasy . . . thickening round us like the spinning of a spider's web. He might have been asking if I wanted more housekeeping money. I put a hand to my head. "I—don't know, Nicholas."

"You—don't—know." His tone brought the blood to my face.

"Nicholas," I said desperately, "try to understand—"

"You were my wife."

"I know, but—"

"You always used to say that you didn't believe in divorce."

"I know," I said again, a little drearily. It was auld lang syne all right. Every quarrel we had ever had, had ended with my being forced on the defensive. I heard the familiar note of excuse creeping into my voice again now, feebly, infuriatingly: "But it wasn't my fault we got divorced."

"Even so, according to what you used to say, you should think of yourself as still bound to me . . . or do you— *now*?"

"Now? I don't follow."

"No? I was harking back to the blond boy friend."

"Damn you, Nicholas!"

He gave me a hard little laugh. "You've got a nasty problem, haven't you, Gianetta? Moral loyalty *versus* civic duty . . . or does the situation simplify itself now into the old love *versus* the new? It would save you a lot of trouble if you could hand me over this minute, wouldn't it?"

The outrage that swept over me was as real, as physical, as shock. I went cold. My voice dropped to a flat icy calm. "If you had been in the lounge just now, you'd have heard Colonel Cowdray-Simpson expressing what happen to be my views. He said that by an act of violence, like murder, a man cuts himself off from his fellows, and forfeits his—his human rights. If I were still your wife"—I put my hands against the wall behind me, feeling for its solid bracing comfort—"if I were still—legally—your wife, I shouldn't help to incriminate you, even if I could, because, as your wife, I should be identified with you in all you did . . . but I would leave you. I couldn't stay with you, knowing you were—"

"Cain?"

"I—yes."

There was an odd note in his voice. "And as it is?"

"As it is—" I stopped, and to my horror my voice caught on a little sob. "As it is," I said raggedly, "I don't know, God damn you. Now let me by."

He moved without a word, and I ran past him, and down the passage to the kitchen.

Chapter 16

In the kitchen there was light, and warmth, and the good smell of food. The cook was busy over the stove, and one of the girls who waited at table was bustling about with stacks of plates.

I hesitated inside the doorway, conscious suddenly of my shaking hands and the tears in my eyes, but Cook looked up, gave me a flushed, fat smile, and pointed to a place set at one end of the big scrubbed table.

"If it's nae odds, mistress," she said in a brisk Lowland voice, "ye can hae yer denner in here. Ye'll get it hetter and quicker. Yon Inspector telt me ye'd want it the noo."

"It's very good of you. I hope it's not too much of a nuisance."

"Nae trouble at all," said Cook comfortably, not moving from the range. "Effie, gie the lady some soup."

Effie was thin and dark, with enormous eyes that devoured me with curiosity. She brought me a plate of steaming soup, putting it down in front of me warily, almost as if I might bite. Then she backed off a step or two, gripping the front of her apron.

"Noo, Effie!" This sharply, from Cook. "Gang awa' intae the dining room wi' the breid!"

Effie went, casting a longing, lingering look behind. As the kitchen door swung to behind her, Cook put down her ladle, and said, in a hoarse, impressive whisper: "Sic a cairry-on, mistress, wi' a' them murrders! It's fair awesome. It garrs yer bluid rin cauld!"

I agreed mechanically. The hot soup was wonderfully comforting, and the bright warmth of the kitchen rapidly helped to dispel the effect of that fantastic little interview in the passage. Cook leaned her plump red fists on the opposite end of the table and regarded me with a sort of professional pleasure.

"Noo, they're grand broth, aren't they?"

"They're—it's excellent, Cook."

"They're pittin' a bit reid intae yer cheeks. Ye looked fair weshed oot and shilpit-like when ye cam' in, I'll say. They were sayin' it was you found her?"

"Yes, I was lucky."

"It was her that was lucky, the puir lassie, to be livin' the day." She nodded heavily. "Mony's the yin that hasnae been sae lucky—and I canna mind a waur simmer."

"Well," I said, "it isn't every year you get—murder."

"No. Guid be thankit. But I wasna' meanin' that." She whipped away my empty soup plate and substituted a lamb chop flanked with peas and roast potatoes. "It was the accidents on the hill I was meanin'."

"Oh?" I remembered something somebody else had said. "Has this year really been worse than usual?"

"Aye, that it has, miss. Thae twa lassies"—she jerked her head vaguely towards the ceiling—"they're the third casualities we've had this season, no' countin' murrders."

"Who were the others?"

"Well, there was a pair frae London—the daft craturs went into the Cuillins wi' neither map nor compass. They were no' fun' till a week after, lyin' at the fit o' a pressy-piece."

"How dreadful! Had the mist come down on them?"

"The day they went up it was as clear as consommay," said Cook. "Naebody kens what happened."

"It's a big price to pay for a bit of carelessness," I said.

"Aye, it's that. But them hills are no' to be taen lightly . . . aye, and that puir man lyin' upstairs, he's mony a time said the verra same, and a grand climber he was an' a'. Aipple tairt."

"I beg your pardon? Oh, I see. Thank you, Cook. This is very good."

"It's no' sae bad," said Cook complacently, watching me sample her rich, flyaway pastry. "Then there was twa o' them students, frae the College at Oxford-and-Cambridge. They baith tummled doon frae a muckle rock—gey near the same bit."

"Dead?"

"Aye, deid as a stane. The rope snappit."

I put my spoon and fork down carefully, side by side, on my empty plate, and stared at them for a moment. But I wasn't seeing them. I was seeing, in a queer fugitive vision, two pairs of climbers climbing in the Cuillin . . . but in each case, another climber moved with them; the third climber, in whose presence ropes snapped, and bodies hurtled to their death. . . .

"A cup o' coffee noo?" suggested Cook.

"I'd love one," I said, "but I think I'd better take it upstairs to drink. The doctors must have finished up there, and Mrs. Persimmon'll want to come down."

"Hoo was the lassie when ye left her?" She set a large blue cup on the table, and began to pour coffee.

"Not too good. But I've a feeling she's going to be all right."

"Thank guidness. I've gien ye the big cup. Ye'd better tak' it quick, while it's warm. Sugar?"

"Please. Thank you very much, Cook. That was excellent. I feel a whole lot better."

"Aye, an' ye look it," said Cook. "Mind ye keep the door lockit the nicht, ma lassie."

"I certainly will," I said fervently, and got up as she turned back to her stove.

There was no one in the passage. I went quickly along it, round the corner with my heart beating a little jerkily, then out into the open hall. Nicholas was there, leaning over the reception desk talking in an undertone to Bill Persimmon. He saw me, but beyond a slight twitch of his black brows he gave no sign. I ignored him, and almost ran up the stairs, balancing my cup of coffee carefully.

I met Mrs. Persimmon and a maid on the landing.

"Oh, there you are, Miss Brooke!" Mrs. Persimmon still sounded harassed, which was hardly surprising. "Did you get some dinner?"

"Yes, thank you, I've done very well."

"Oh, good, good. Well, the police are expecting you now, I think."

"How's Miss Symes?"

"I hardly know. Still unconscious, and the doctor won't say very much. Oh dear, oh dear. . . ." And she plunged downstairs, followed by the maid laden with crumpled linen. I heard her still lamenting faintly as I went along to my room and knocked on the door.

The Inspector opened it.

"Ah, Miss Brooke. Come away in."

He shut the door carefully behind me. The doctor had gone. Roberta, in her blankets, looked very white and still, so white that I exclaimed anxiously: "Inspector Mackenzie, is she all right?"

He nodded. "The doctor thinks so. He says she'll pull through."

"That's wonderful!"

His eye was on Roberta's quiet, shuttered face. "Aye," he said, his voice expressionless. Then he turned to me. "And you? Did you get some food?"

"Yes. Cook fed me in the kitchen."

"Good. How do you feel now?"

I smiled. "Ready for anything—But I hope you're going to tell me what to do, before I'm left alone with the patient."

"The doctor left instructions, and I wrote them down for you." He indicated a paper on the bedside table. "But it's mostly a case of keeping the hot bottles filled and the room warm. You can give her a little broth, or tea with a dash of brandy in, whenever she'll take it. The doctor had a confinement due, so he had to go, but if you get at all worried, you can get hold of me, and I'll ring up the Broadford hospital for advice."

"D'you mean I'm to send Neill for you?"

"No. Use the telephone. I'm using Miss Maling's room. I'll probably be up most of the night, but when I do go upstairs, I'll switch it through to there. Don't hesitate to ring up if you're in the least nervous or worried. We'll be about all night."

"I won't."

"Good. Well, now"—he turned to Neill, who had appeared in the doorway—"Neill, you know what to do. Make yourself comfortable. Sergeant Munro'll relieve you at two o'clock, and I'll be along myself now and again to see everything's all right. I doubt if any of us'll get much sleep tonight." He crossed to the window and stood looking out. "There's a mist coming up. A pity. It's never a help on this kind of job. I think. . . ." He reached a hand up and latched the window shut. "That disposes of *that*. D'you mind being a trifle stuffy?"

"Under the circumstances, not at all."

"That's all right, then. Well, I'll leave you. I'm afraid you've a long night ahead of you, but I think it's a safe night. And—oh, yes, Major Persimmon is to keep the dynamo running all night, so the lights will be on. All right, Neill?"

"Yes, sir."

He turned to me. "Are you a light sleeper, lassie?"

"I think so."

"There's no need for you to stay awake all night, you know. She'll sleep, and if she wants you, Neill will wake you. Get some rest yourself between whiles. Right?"

"Right."

"Well, good night, lassie."

"Inspector Mackenzie—"

He was already at the door. He turned with his hand on the knob. "Yes?"

"There are some things—I have a few things you ought to know."

"Important?"

"I—I'm not sure."

"Anything that'll enable me to arrest our murderer here and now?"

"Oh no. No."

His eyes considered me, queerly. "You've located him, haven't you?"

"*No!*" The single syllable came violently, surprising me as much as the Inspector.

He looked at me for a moment. "Then I dare say it'll keep till morning, ma'am," he said.

He went out. I went quickly across the room and turned the key. The whirr and click of the wards was reassuring, and the *chock* as the bolt slid home punctuated our security with sharp finality.

Chapter 17

THE LONG EVENING dragged through and the night came. I nodded over the fire with *The Bride of Lammermoor*, fighting off the feeling of desperate tiredness that threatened to overwhelm me. Neill sat in the shadows beside Roberta's bed, his long body still and relaxed in the wicker chair, his back to me and the rest of the room. Roberta stirred once or twice, but her breathing seemed every moment more natural and her color improved, so that it was with a reasonably quiet mind that I eventually put down my book and decided to try to get some sleep.

I crossed the room softly towards my bed. "Good night, Neill."

"Good night, miss," he answered, without turning his head, and, absurdly enough, I felt a wave of relief pass over me at the quiet reply. It was as if one of the still shadows of the room had offered reassurance; and it brought home to me the unwelcome realization that, in spite of all precautions, in spite of Neill's very presence, I was really very nervous indeed. I chided myself sharply as I wound up my little bedside clock and slid my feet out of my slippers. The room was locked, door and window, and Neill, solid dependable Neill, was here with me; and there, at arm's length, on the other end of the telephone, was Inspector Mackenzie.

I turned back the eiderdown and crept underneath it, wrapping the full skirt of my housecoat round me. My whole body ached with weariness, but I had no fear that I should sleep too soundly to hear Roberta moving. There were other fears that would keep me too near the edge of consciousness for that. . . .

I was quite right. I dozed and waked, and dozed again —little uneasy snatches of sleep that might have been of a minute's or of an hour's duration. Twice, Roberta stirred and whimpered and had me up on my elbow in a flash; but each time she subsided once more into sleep. Once, some time soon after midnight, she seemed to rouse more fully, so I got up and heated broth, and Neill and I managed to make her swallow half a dozen spoonfuls before she turned her head away with a tiny petulant movement, and subsided again into sleep. Another time I remember boiling more water for bottles, and I recollect, dimly, the quiet change-over of watchers, as Hector Munro relieved Neill at two o'clock; and I remember twice, as in a recurrent dream, the Inspector's voice outside the locked door, asking how we did. Some time during the dead hours Hecky made a cup of tea—strong, this time—and I drank it curled up warmly under my eiderdown before I got up yet again to fill hotwater bottles.

I did my job efficiently enough, I know, but I must have moved through that firelit fantasy in a state suspended between wakefulness and dream, so that, looking back now, I can hardly tell where the reality ended and the nightmare began. Indeed, my memory now is of a night of continuous nightmare, where the ordinariness of the tasks which engaged me could not hold at bay the shadows haunting, uneasily, the corners of the firelit room. The ticking of my little clock, the workaday hum of the singing kettle—these homely sounds became, to me lying dozing through the small, crawling hours, distorted into the very stuff of nightmare—manifestations as eerie and terror-filled as the shadows that gibbered across the fire-flickering ceiling above my head. Shadows and fire . . . shadows across the glare . . . shadows coalescing even as I watched into the image of a murderer gesticulating before the flames, dancing crazily round a pyre that grew and swelled and dilated into a gigantic smoking shape, a red-hot Paracutin of a bonfire, a veritable hell's mountain. . . . And now it was Blaven itself that loomed over me, lit with flames. And a solitary, faceless climber straddled that devil's gully, pulling after him a length of cut rope. Somewhere, a knife gleamed, and I heard the soft stutter of two voices in counterpoint, wavering through the sound of falling water. . . . *You used to be my wife. . . . You've located him, haven't you? . . . You've got a nasty problem, haven't you? . . . You've located him, haven't you? . . . haven't you? . . .*

My own "No!" woke me finally, with such a jerk that I wondered if I had spoken aloud, and strained my ears for the vibration of my own voice among the shadows. Or was it Hecky who had spoken? Or Roberta? I pushed myself up onto my elbow and looked across at her. She was moving, making fretful little noises of pain, but it was not this that made my heart jump and my body stiffen in its little nest under the eiderdown. Hecky wasn't there.

Even as I reacted to this in a manner that betrayed the lamentable state of my nerves, I turned my head and saw him, like the specter of my dream, in front of the fire. But this fire threw no terrifying shadow back into the room, and for the worst of reasons. It was almost out.

A glance at my clock told me that it was quarter past four. I had not been asleep long, and Hecky had presumably not been to sleep at all, but in spite of us the peat fire, inexpertly stacked, had dwindled and died into an inert-looking mass of black sods.

Now a peat fire is a tricky thing for an amateur to manage. Once it is going well, it is wonderfully hot, a red glowing mass like the heart of a blast furnace. Mrs. Persimmon had banked this one expertly, and Neill, too, had known what to do with it, but Hecky was a townsman and a Lowlander, while I was the most helpless of amateurs. Between us we must have handled it very clumsily, for it had burned itself almost out, and as Hecky stirred it the peat crumbled, and fell away into fragments that rapidly began to blacken.

I swung myself off the bed, thrust my feet into my slippers, and went softly across to the fireplace.

"Won't it go at all, Sergeant?"

"It will not."

"Isn't there any more peat?"

"Och, yes, there's plenty. It's the putting it on that's tricky. Have you the way of it at all, miss?"

"Far from it, but we've got to try." There was a small pile of fresh peats on the hearth. I knelt down beside Hecky and together we stacked them over the embers and tried to blow them to a flame. But to no avail; the red ash waned and darkened, and the peats steamed sullenly, black and unresponsive. The room felt cold.

"It's no good," I said. "It's going out."

We looked at one another in some dismay, then I stood up, biting my lip. I had to put fresh bottles in Roberta's bed. I had to be ready to make her another drink. I had to get the room warm against the chill hours of daybreak.

"I'm sorry," said Hecky. "I—"

"It's my fault as much as yours. In fact, neither of us is to blame if we can't manage the dashed thing. What we should have done is to ask Mrs. Persimmon for some wood to help us keep it going. I'm afraid it didn't occur to me."

He stood up, dusting his hands lightly together. "Will I get Inspector Mackenzie to bring some wood, then?"

"There should be some somewhere," I said. "The lounge fire was made up with logs, I remember. Perhaps—"

"I ken fine where it is." He was at the telephone now. "We've been all over this place at one time and another, you'll mind. It's oot the back." . . . He put the receiver back and looked at me. "No answer. He'll be taking a look around, likely enough."

"Then—had we better wait?"

He glanced at the black fireplace. "That'll be oot in five minutes. I'd best go myself."

I said doubtfully: "Should you, d'you think?"

"You've got to get this fire going, have ye no'?"

"Yes. Yes, I have."

"Well, then, I reckon I'd better go. And if you don't open the door till I get back, there'll be no harm done."

"I—I suppose not. How am I going to be sure it's you when you come back?"

"I'll knock—this way." He moved nearer. His hand went out to the mantelpiece beside me. A finger fluttered. I heard a tiny tapping, the sort that might be made by a grasshopper's feet landing a little raggedly on a leaf: *tap—taptap—taptaptap—tap.* . . . Nobody else but I, with my ear some nine inches away, could possibly have heard it.

"Right," I said. "Don't be long, for goodness' sake. And—oh, Sergeant—"

"Yes, miss?"

"If there's a kettle hot on the stove, you might bring it up. It'll save time."

"O.K., miss."

"You—you'll be all right?"

He grinned down at me. "Don't worry about me, now. I'd give a year's pay to meet that chap, whoever he is, down by the woodshed! I'll no' be more than five minutes, miss, and if I see Inspector Mackenzie prowling around, I'll send him along."

He let himself out, and I locked and bolted the door again behind him. I heard him go softly down the passage. Silence.

My heart was beating uncomfortably hard, and once again I had to take myself sharply to task. I turned resolutely from the door, and went over to have a look at Roberta. She seemed to have relaxed a little, and her breathing was less shallow, but her eyelids twitched from time to time, as if the light troubled her. I took my green silk scarf out of a drawer and dropped it over her bedside light, then went back to nurse my little core of red fire till Hecky should come back.

He was surprisingly quick. I had ripped some pages from the *Autocar* and with these and some small crumblings of peat, was getting a nice little lick of flame, when I heard the soft tap at the door.

I was halfway across the room before I realized that the sound had not been the grasshopper tapping that Hecky and I had arranged.

It came again, a tiny sound: *Tap-tap-tap.*

I was standing three feet from the door, with my hands, in rigid fists, pressed down against the front of my thighs. My heart began to jerk in slow, sickening thuds. I stood, turned to marble, with my eyes on the door, while the seconds ticked madly by on the little bedside clock.

Ever so gently, the door handle turned. Ever so softly, the door rattled as somebody pressed against it.

If I screamed, I thought, people would wake up, and they would catch him there . . . the murderer, trying to get at Roberta.

But if I screamed, it might penetrate that still slumber of Roberta's and I had no idea of the possible effect of such a shock. It was not a risk that I felt I had any right to take.

Then I was at the door.

"Hullo?" I was surprised that my voice sounded so normal. "Is that you, Sergeant?"

Of course it wasn't; but if he said it was. . . .

"No." The vigorous whisper was certainly not Hecky's. "It's Inspector Mackenzie. I came to take a look at her. Open up, will you, lassie?"

Even as I accepted the statement with a quick uprush of relief, I surprised myself again. I heard my voice saying calmly: "Just a minute, Inspector. I'll get a dressing gown on."

In three strides I was at the telephone, and had lifted the receiver. My little clock chittered the seconds crazily away beside me ... two, four, seven seconds, seven dragging light-years before I heard the *click* of the other receiver being lifted, and Inspector Mackenzie's voice, soft but alert, saying sharply: "Mackenzie here. What is it?"

I cupped a hand round the mouthpiece and whispered into it: "Come quickly! *Quickly! He's at the door!*"

The line went dead. My knees gave way under me, and I sat down slowly on my bed, with the receiver still clutched in my hand. My head turned, stiff as a doll's head, to watch the door.

There was no sound, no rattle, no movement of the handle. The door stood blind, bland in its smooth white paint, telling nothing.

There was a swift stealthy rush of feet up the corridor. A voice.

"Inspector? Is anything the matter?"

"Where the devil have you been, Hector Munro?"

"To get wood. I'm sorry, sir. Is something wrong?"

Doors opened. I heard Hartley Corrigan's voice, raw-edged with nerves. "What the devil's going on here?" Then his wife's scared whisper: "Has something—happened?"

"Nothing, madam. Please go back to bed." The Inspector's voice sank to a reassuring mumble, and, since I could now hear three or four voices murmuring in the corridor, I opened my door.

The Corrigans were just withdrawing into their room, which was opposite my own. The only other people who seemed to have been disturbed were Colonel Cowdray-Simpson and Hubert Hay, whose rooms were just round the corner from our passage, in the main corridor. As I opened the door, Hecky, standing rather shamefacedly before the Inspector with a bundle of wood under one arm and a still-steaming kettle in the other, turned and saw me, and came hurrying down the passage in some relief.

Inspector Mackenzie whipped round after him. His voice was still low, but clear and urgent.

"Hecky! Don't touch that door! Miss Brooke, stand away from the door, please."

"Look here, Inspector"—this was Colonel Cowdray-

Simpson, still surprisingly authoritative in a deplorable old dressing gown, and without his teeth—"what's wrong?"

"Please accept my assurance that there's nothing wrong, sir. You can reassure Mrs. Cowdray-Simpson. And you, Mr. Hay. I promise you that if I want help I'll ask for it, but just at the moment—"

"O.K. I'm off." And Hubert Hay, resplendent in Paisley silk disappeared reluctantly.

The Inspector came swiftly down to where I was still standing. "Now, what's all this?"

It was so much the conventional policeman's opening that I felt an absurd desire to laugh. I said, shakily: "He—he was at the door. The murderer. He said—he said—"

He took my arm and drew me gently into the room towards my bed.

"You sit down there. Don't try to talk." He shot a rapid glance at Roberta, and was apparently satisfied. "Hecky, get that fire going. . . . No, on second thoughts, let me do it. You go to my room and get my bag and give that door a going-over." He looked at me. "You said he was at the door. I suppose he touched it?"

"Yes. He pushed it, and turned the knob."

He gave a small grunt of satisfaction. "The knob, Hecky. No, man, leave it standing open, then no ghosts can wipe it clean before you come back. Aah!"

This was an exclamation of satisfaction as the dry sticks caught alight, and the flames roared up the chimney in a crackling blaze.

"I suppose there wasn't a sign of anybody when you came?" I said.

"No." He was expertly stacking peat.

"He must have heard me telephoning you. I'm sorry."

"On the contrary, you did very well."

"Well, I'm sorry I made Hecky go downstairs, then. It was my fault for letting the fire down, but I had to get it going again."

He pushed the kettle down among the now blazing peats, and stood up. "It might have been a lucky stroke," he said, "if we *had* seen the murderer. Now, supposing you tell me what happened."

I told him about it, while Hecky busied himself over the surface of the door, and Roberta lay quietly in her blankets in the little green glow of the bedside lamp.

He listened in silence, his eyes on my face. "Hum," he said at length. "He must either have heard Hecky go, or have seen him go out across the yard. It doesn't get us much forrarder, except for one thing."

"What's that?"

"It proves that Miss Symes can convict him. He was our third climber, all right. He cut that rope."

I said flatly. "Inspector, do you know who this murderer is?"

"Have you finished, Hecky?"

"Aye, sir. Juist aboot it."

"Inspector, please—"

"Any luck, Hecky?"

Hecky straightened up. His face was rueful. "No, sir. It's been wiped."

"What?" The Inspector was across the room in three strides, and was examining the door. His mouth was thin and hard. "Damn!" he said explosively, then added: "'All right, Hecky. Shut the door and get back to your chair." He came back into the room looking angry. "Bang goes my proof," he said bitterly.

"Proof?" I said. "Then you *do* know who it is?"

"Know. Hardly that, perhaps. Call it a pretty sure guess. . . . But a guess is no good to a policeman, and we've no proof at all—not a shred; and if yon lassie on the bed doesn't open her mouth soon. I'm afraid of what may happen. Look at tonight, for instance. Look at the kind of chance he takes—and might very well get away with, God help us, because nobody in their right senses would expect him to take a risk like that."

"He'll tempt his luck once too often," I said.

"Luck!" His voice seemed to explode on the word. "He murders Heather Macrae with a twenty-foot blaze of fire on the open side of Blaven. He kills Miss Bradford in full sight of Camasunary glen in the middle of the afternoon. He cuts Beagle's throat within yards—*yards*—of witnesses. And now this!" He looked at me, and added quietly: "I've been on this corridor all night. I only went downstairs to the office twenty minutes ago. And then—only then—your fire goes out, and he sees Hecky Munro going off and leaving you alone."

"I—I'm sorry," I said feebly.

He smiled at her. "Don't say that, lassie, I told you it wasn't your fault. You've been quite a useful recruit to the

Force, indeed you have. . . . That kettle's boiling. Shall I do those for you?"

"I can manage, thanks." I began to fill Roberta's bottles.

He was standing by her bed, staring down at her face as if he would draw her secret from behind the pale barrier of her brow. His own forehead was creased, his hair tousled, his chin grey with unshaven stubble. His fists were thrust deep into his pockets, and his shoulders were rounded. He looked like any worried middle-aged man wakened out of sleep by the baby's wailing. Then he turned his head, and the quiet intelligent eyes gave the picture the lie. "Do you mind finishing your watch now?"

"No."

"Don't send Hecky away any more."

"I certainly won't!"

"I shan't be on the end of the telephone. I have—a few things to do. But don't worry. And who knows, it may all be over sooner than you think. We'll get him. Oh yes, we'll get him. . . ." And his eyes were no longer kind, but cold and frightening.

Chapter 18

WHEN, ONCE AGAIN, I had locked and bolted the door behind him, I busied myself over Roberta. It was a full twenty minutes before I had finished my tasks, and, when I had done, all desire for sleep had gone.

I drew a curtain aside and looked out of the window. It was still misty. I could see the faint grey of the first morning light filtering hazily through the veil like light through a pearl. It looked dank and chilly, and I was glad to be able to turn back to the firelit room.

Hecky had made more tea, and I took a cup back to bed with me, wishing yet again that I had something reasonable to read. At this hour of the morning, my heart failed me at the thought of *The Bride of Lammermoor,* and I had torn up most of the *Autocars* to light the fire. There remained *The Golden Bough*—an odd thing, surely, to find in a remote hotel in Scotland? It was a pleasant

title, I thought, but I had a vague feeling that it was as
heavy going, in its own way, as *The Bride of Lammermoor*.
Something to do with primitive religions ... hardly a bedside book, and hardly, I thought, picking it up incuriously,
the sort of book with which to while away even the wettest
day in Skye. Except, of course, Sunday, when there was
no fishing.

But someone had been reading it. There was a book-
mark, an old envelope, thrust between the pages, and, of
its own accord, the heavy book fell open at the place thus
marked. It opened in the ready and accustomed manner of
a book much handled at that particular page.

I looked at it, mildly curious.

The Beltane Fires, I read. *In the Central Highlands of
Scotland bonfires, known as the Beltane fires, were form-
erly kindled with great ceremony on the first of May, and
traces of human sacrifices at them were particularly clear
and unequivocal.* . . .

I sat up, staring unbelievingly at the page, my brain
whirling. It was as if the words had exploded into the
silence of the room, and I glanced across at Hecky Munro's broad back, hardly able to believe that he could be
unconscious of their impact. My eye skipped down the cold,
precise print. From it, as they had been scrawled in luminous paint, words and phrases leapt out at me. . . . *Their
sacrifices were therefore offered in the open air, frequently
upon the tops of hills ... a pile of wood or other fuel ...
in the islands of Skye, Mull and Tiree ... they applied a
species of agarie which grows on old birch trees and is
very combustible.* . . .

There flashed between me and the printed page a vivid
memory: the birch grove, silver gilt and summer lace, with
broken pieces of fungus still littering the wet ground between the smooth-skinned trees. And the brown fans of
agaric pushing, palms up, from some of the sleek boles.
Very combustible. . . .

I read on, the cool detached prose bringing to my racing
mind picture after picture: *in the Hebrides, in Wales, in
Ireland*—in the queer Celtic corners of the land those fires
were lit, and rites were performed that echoed grotesquely,
though innocently, the grim and bloody rites of an older
day. May-day fires, Midsummer fires, Hallowe'en fires—
for countless years these had purified the ground, protected
the cattle from plague, burned the witches. . . .

Burned the witches. Another memory swam up, sickeningly: a young girl lying in the embers with her throat cut; Hubert Hay's voice talking of magic and folklore and writers who questioned Heather Macrae about old superstitions.

I found that my hands were wet with perspiration, and the print was seesawing in front of my eyes. It was absurd. *Absurd.* No modern young woman of eighteen, even if she did live in a lonely corner of the earth, was going to be sacrificed as a witch. *That* part of it was nonsense, anyway. But why had she been killed, then, and in that unmistakably ritual manner? Hardly in order to protect the crops. Even James Farlane, born and bred in the mountains, could no longer believe—

I jerked myself out of my thoughts, and read on. I read how, when the sacrificial fire was built, it was lighted, not from "tame" fire, but from new fire, "needfire," the living wildfire struck afresh from dry oak, and fed with wild agaric. I read how those who struck the living fire "would turn their pockets inside out, and see that every piece of money and all metals were off their persons." I read how, in some localities, the one who made the wildfire must be young and chaste. . . .

The print swam away from me finally then in a wild and drowning dance of words. I put my hands to my face and thought, in a slow painful enlightenment, of Heather Macrae, who was young and chaste, and who divested herself of her pathetic little gewgaws to make the needfire for her murderer. She must have thought the whole affair crazy, I mused bitterly, but she thought it was fun, it was "different," it was the sort of romantic craziness that a clever bookish gentleman from London might indulge in.

My thoughts skidded away from that same clever gentleman from London, as I tried, vainly, to fit the other killings into the same framework of primitive ritual. Where, in the plans of this primeval throwback of a murderer, did Beagle's murder fit? Or Marion Bradford's cut rope? Or the students from Oxford and Cambridge? Or Marcia Maling's doll?

It became more than ever certain, on the evidence of this book, that the only kind of logic that could knit together crimes so various must be the cracked logic of madness. And that the book was evidence there was no doubt. There were too many parallels between its calm statements and the crazy ritual murder on Blaven hill. Nor could it be mere coincidence that the book itself was here, in this hotel. There was the probability that it was the murderer's own: a man whose studies had made him sufficiently familiar with such rites and customs—a man of unstable mind —might, when that mind finally overturned, wallow in just such a blotched travesty of ritual as Heather's murder now showed itself to be. Or it was possible—

I was, I found, still clutching in my damp fist the crumpled envelope that had marked the page. My hand shook a little as I smoothed it out.

I sat looking at it for a very long time.

The envelope was in my father's handwriting. It had no stamp, but it bore, in his clear, beautiful hand, a name and address:

> *Nicholas Drury, Esq.,*
> *at the Camas Fhionnaridh Hotel,*
> *Isle of Skye,*
> *Inverness-shire.*

Chapter 19

THE MORNING brought misty sunshine and the nurse. She was a youngish, square-built woman, who looked kind and immensely capable. With relief I abandoned Roberta to her and went down to breakfast.

As I went into the dining room, heads turned, and Mrs. Cowdray-Simpson asked quickly: "The girl—how is she?"

I smiled. "All right so far, thank you. The nurse is with her now, and says she's getting on well."

"I'm so glad! I was so afraid that all that disturbance in the night—"

"It was nothing," I said. "I let the fire out, and the Inspector heard Sergeant Munro prowling down the stairs to get wood for me."

Nobody else spoke to me while I ate my breakfast, for which I was grateful. I found myself being careful not to catch anybody's eye. I had just poured my second cup of coffee when Effie, round-eyed, appeared at my elbow.

"If you please, miss, the Inspector says—when you're ready, he says, but not to be interrupting yourself—"

Her voice was high-pitched and possessed remarkable carrying power. It was into a dead and listening silence that I replied: "I'll go and see the Inspector at once. Thank you, Effie."

I picked up *The Golden Bough*, which I had wrapped in yet another piece of *The Autocar*, took my cup of coffee in the other hand, and walked out of the dining room, still in that uncomfortable silence. My face was flaming. Last night's quarantine seemed still to be isolating me, Nicholas's mocking phrase to be whispering me out of the room. In each look that followed me I could sense the same resentment. In one pair of eyes there might also be fear. My cheeks were still flying scarlet banners when I got to the Inspector's temporary office.

He greeted me cheerfully, with a shrewd glance at my face which provoked me into saying, tartly: "I could do without the distinction of not being a suspect, Inspector Mackenzie!"

He was unperturbed. "Is that so? Don't they like it?"

"Of course they don't! I feel—cut off . . . and the funny thing is that it's *I* who feel guilty. I wish it was all over!"

"I'm with you there." He stretched out a hand. "Is that for me?"

I handed him *The Golden Bough*. In some curious way I felt that, by doing so, I had committed myself to something, had started down a path from which there was no turning back. I sat down. "I've marked the place," I said.

I bent my head over my coffee cup, stirring it unnecessarily, concentrating on the brown swirl of the liquid against the blue sides of the cup. I heard the Inspector make an odd little sound, then he said sharply: "Where did you find this?"

I told him.

"And when did you see this marked section?"

"Last night." I told him about that, too. But not about the crumpled envelope. It was in my pocket. I could not go quite so far down the path. Not yet.

"It was you who marked the passages?"

"Yes."

"Do you know whose book this is?"

The envelope burned in my pocket. "No."

There was a pause. I looked up to find his eyes watching me. He said: "You had other things to tell me, I believe. You told me so, before you found this book. Now, Miss Brooke"—he was being very formal this morning—"what is it that you think I ought to know?"

"The first thing," I said, "concerns the cut climbing rope that killed Marion Bradford."

"Yes?"

I began to tell him about my trip downstairs in the darkness on my first night in the hotel, and how both Jamesy Farlane and Alastair Braine had been in the hotel porch.

"And Mr. Corrigan had been fishing with them," I said slowly. "Alastair said he'd already come back—but yesterday his wife said he didn't get in that night till three o'clock. It was about half past two when I spoke to Alastair."

The inspector was writing rapidly. He looked up when I felt silent. "What you're trying to tell me is that each one of these three men had the opportunity to damage the girls' climbing rope the night before the climb."

"Yes," I said, miserably.

"Then where does Dougal Macrae's third climber come in?"

"He might be innocent," I said, "and just be frightened! When he saw them fall—"

"Aye, aye, lassie," said the Inspector drily, and, again gave me that long considering look. "And had you anything else to tell me?"

I hesitated. The envelope? Not yet, I told myself, not yet, . . . And the other thing? The half-lie I had told about what happened by the second bonfire? It wasn't proof, I assured myself desperately, and proof was all he wanted. Surely I didn't have to tell him? Not yet. . . . He was watching me steadily across the table. I began rather hurriedly to tell him about the episode of Marcia's doll. Finally I sat back, and looked unhappily across the table at him. "But perhaps you knew?"

He nodded. "Mrs. Persimmon told me about that. But you can forget it. It's not a mystery any longer, and it never was a piece of this mystery in any case. I think I may tell you that it was part of a little private feud between Mrs. Corrigan and Miss Maling."

"Oh? You mean *Alma Corrigan* did it?"

"Yes. She told me this morning. She did it to frighten

Miss Maling away from the hotel for—er, reasons of her own."

"I—see." I was remembering Alma Corrigan's face as she watched Marcia's car driving away across the glen. "Well, it appears to have worked."

His mouth relaxed a little. "Quite so." Then he looked down at his notes. "Well, I'm much obliged to you for telling me these things. I think you were right to do so. Is there anything else?"

"No," I said, but I was not well enough guarded yet, and his eyes lifted quickly to my face. They had sharpened with interest.

He said flatly: "You're lying to me, aren't you? There is something else."

"No." But I said it too loudly.

He looked at me very gravely for a few long seconds. Then he laid the pencil carefully down on his papers, and put his hands, palm downwards, flat on the desk. "Lassie" —his tone was no longer official; it was very kind—"I think you told me a lie last night, didn't you?"

"I? A lie? What—"

"When you said you hadn't guessed who the murderer was."

I bit my lip and sat rigid, my eyes on the floor.

He said: "Do you really think a woman of Marion Bradford's experience wouldn't have noticed if the rope was damaged when she put it on? Do you really think that rope was cut in the hotel porch that night?"

"I—it might have been."

"It might. But you don't think it was."

"N—no."

He paused. "I'll tell you how we think this murder was done," he said at length. "You realized, of course, that Roberta Symes never climbed across the Sputan Dhu at all?"

He added, as I stared at him: "There was no rope on her body, was there?"

I said slowly. "No. No, there wasn't. Of course . . . if she'd been middle man on the rope the murderer *couldn't* have cut it between her and Marion. D'you know, I never worked that out? How stupid of me!"

"It's just as well you didn't, or you'd have left the Sputan Dhu to look for her elsewhere."

"What did happen, then?"

"We think he offered to do the climb with Marion Bradford, Roberta watching. When he got Miss Bradford to the one pitch that's out of sight of the other side—there's an overhang—"

"I know. I noticed it. He could have cut the rope then without being seen."

He nodded. "He pulled her off and cut the rope. Roberta would see an 'accident,' see her fall. Then she would hear him shout that he was coming back. He could get back quite easily alone by going higher above the gully. She would wait for him in who knows what agony of mind, there by the gully's edge. And in her turn, when he came there, he would throw her down. She must have fallen out of sight, or, if he'd suspected she wasn't dead, he'd have gone down to finish her."

I said nothing. I couldn't speak, couldn't think. I believe I shut my eyes. I know I was trembling.

"Lassie," he said, very gently, "if a man's a murderer, and a murderer like this one, crazy and—yes, vicious and crazy, he's not fit to defend, you know."

I said chokily: "Loyalty—"

"Doesn't enter into it. He's an outlaw. Your loyalty is to the rest of us, the sane ordinary people who want him locked up so that they can be safe."

"Well, why don't you arrest him, if you're so sure?"

"I told you. I can't possibly move without proof. I'm waiting for some information to come from London. Or—there's Roberta."

"Why did you leave me with her, if you're so sure I'd shield the murderer?" I cried.

"Because I'm a good enough judge of people to know that, when it comes to the point, you'll be on the right side, whatever your—loyalties."

"My instincts, you mean," I said bitterly. "If you'd been in the lounge last night, you'd have heard me talking very fine and large about my principles, but now—" I got up. "Has no one ever told you that people mean more to women than principles? I'm a woman, Inspector Mackenzie."

He had risen, and his eyes met mine levelly. "So was Heather Macrae."

I blazed at him at that. "I don't know why you're treating me to a sermon on loyalty, Inspector Mackenzie! Even

if I *did* guess who your murderer was it's only a guess! How
am I supposed to be able to help you catch him? I've told
you everything—"

"No." His voice was soft, but it brought me up short.
"I still don't believe you." He surveyed me grimly. "And
if this fact—whatever it is—that you are keeping back, is
one that will give me the proof I want, then I must warn
you—"

"Proof? I haven't any proof! I swear I haven't! And if I
had—oh God, I must have time to think," I said shakily,
and almost ran out of the room.

There may have been people in the hall; I never saw
them. I went blindly across it, making without coherent
thought for the glass porch, and the fresh air and freedom
of the glen. But when I pushed my way through the swing
doors into the porch I came face to face with Dougal
Macrae coming in. He greeted me gravely.

"Good morning, mistress. It's a grand morning for it,
forby at bit of mist coming up frae the bay. Are you wanting to go right away?"

"Go?" I looked at him blankly.

"It was today I was taking you fishing, Mistress Brooke.
Had you forgotten?"

"Fishing? Oh—" I began to laugh, rather weakly, and
then apologized. "I'm sorry; but it seems odd to be thinking
of fishing after—after all this."

"To be sure it does. But ye canna juist be sitting round
to wait for what's going to happen, mistress. Ye'll be better
out in the clear air fishing the Abhainn Camas Fhionnaridh and taking your mind off things. Fine I know it."

"Yes, I suppose you do. . . . All right, Mr. Macrae, I'll
come. Give me five minutes."

Three-quarters of an hour later, as I stood on the
heather where the Camasunary River flows out of Loch na
Creitheach, I knew that Dougal had been right.

The mist that, earlier that morning, had blanketed the
glen, had now lifted and rolled back, to lie in long vapor
veils on the lower slopes of Blaven and Sgurr na Stri. Just
beside us, An't Sròn was all but invisible in its shroud, and
from its feet the loch stretched northwards, pale-glimmer-
ing, to merge with the mist above it in a shifting opalescent
haze. Marsco had vanished; the Cuillin had withdrawn behind the same invisible cloak, but directly above our heads

the sky was blue and clear, and the sun shone warmly down. The river, sliding out of the loch in a great slithering fan of silver, narrowed where we stood into a deeper channel, wrangling and glittering among boulders that broke it into foam or shouldered it up in glossy curves for all the world like the backs of leaping salmon. Close under the banks, in the little backwaters, piles of froth bobbed and swayed on water brown as beer. The smell of drying heather and peaty water, strong and fresh, was laced with the pungent odor of bog myrtle.

Dougal was a good instructor. He soon showed me how to assemble my hired rod, how to fix the reel and tie the fly, and then, with infinite patience, he began to teach me how to cast. Neither of us spoke a word about anything but the matter in hand, and very few, even, about that. It was not long before I found, to my own surprise, that the difficult art I was attempting had, indeed, a powerful fascination, before which the past faded, the future receded, and the whole of experience narrowed down to this stretch of glancing, glimmering water, and the fly I was trying to cast across it. The timeless scene and the eternal voice of the water created between them a powerful hypnosis under whose influence the hotel with its inmates and its problems seemed far away and relatively unimportant.

And even if my own problem did not recede with the others, it did—so passionately did I refuse to face it—relax a little of its clawhold on my mind.

Dougal had put up his own rod, but did not at first use it. He sat on the bank, smoking and watching me, occasionally getting up to demonstrate a cast. Of course I never caught anything; I did not get even the suspicion of a bite. But so powerfully had the peace and timelessness of the place worked upon me that when at length Dougal began to unwrap sandwiches for lunch I was able to think and speak with tolerable composure.

We ate at first in silence, while the water ran bubbling-brown past our feet, and a dipper flew zit-zitting up and down the center of the river. A fish leaped in a flashing silver arc.

"That's just where I was fishing," I said humbly. "I must have been casting over him all the time, and never caught him."

"You might yet. I've known stranger things happen,"

said Dougal. It could hardly be called an encouraging answer, but I supposed that, from a Highlander, it might even be accounted praise. He looked up at the sky. "It's a bit overbright for the fish, in fact. If the mist came down a little, and took some of the glare off, it might be better."

"It seems a pity to wish the sun away."

"You'll not notice, once you're fishing again."

We finished our lunch in silence, then Dougal got out his ancient pipe, while I fished in my pocket for cigarettes. As my fingers closed over the remains of yesterday's rather battered packet of Players, they encountered something else, something metallic and unfamiliar.

I gave an exclamation as I remembered what it was. Dougal turned an inquiring eye in my direction, through a small fog of pipe smoke.

"I ought to have given this to the Inspector, I suppose," I said, withdrawing my hand from my pocket with the cairngorm brooch. "I'd forgotten all about it. It's Roberta's, and—"

"*Where did ye get that?*" The big Scotsman's voice was harsh. His pipe fell unheeded into the heather, and his hand shot out and grabbed the brooch from my palm. He turned it over and over in a hand that shook.

"Why—up on the hill, yesterday," I said, uncertainly. "On the scree near the Sputan Dhu. I—I thought Miss Symes must have dropped it there."

"It was Heather's." Dougal's voice was unsteady too.

"*Heather's?*" Confusedly I tried to remember where I had picked it up. . . . Yes, it had been lying on the scree below the ledge where she had been found. Could it have dropped or been kicked off that little pile of metal in the corner? . . . I turned to look back at Blaven, only to find that the mist was, indeed, rolling down the slopes behind us like a tide of smoking lava. Blaven was already invisible, and a great wall of mist bore steadily across the glen behind us, obliterating the afternoon.

"I gave it to her for her birthday," said Dougal, his voice unnaturally loud and harsh. "She was wearing it when she went out that night. . . ." He stared at it for a moment longer, then thrust it back at me. "You'd best take it, mistress. Give it to the Inspector and tell him where you found it. God knows it won't help him, but—" He broke off, and turned with bent head to hunt for his pipe. By the time he had got it alight again his face was once more impassive, and his hands steady. He glanced round at the silently advancing mist.

"This'll be better for the fish," he said, and relapsed into silence.

The sun had gone, and with it, the peace of the place had vanished too. The finding of that pathetic brooch had brought back, only too vividly, the horrors which had beset this lovely glen. My own miserable doubts and fears began again to press in on me as the grey mist was pressing. The other side of the river was invisible now. We seemed, Dougal and I, to be in the center of a world of rolling grey cloud, islanded between the loud river and the lake, whose still and somber glimmer dwinded, by degrees, into a grey haze of nothing.

I shivered. "Don't you think we ought to go back, Mr. Macrae? I think I ought to give the brooch to the Inspector straightaway."

He got up. "It's as you wish, mistress. Shall I take down the rods, then?"

I hesitated. Perhaps it was only the eeriness of the mist-wrapped glen, but, suddenly, violently, I wanted to be gone. I could escape this thing no longer; I must face my problem now, and take whatever uneasy peace was left to me.

"We must go back," I said at length. "There are—other reasons—why I should see the Inspector. I mustn't put it off any more. And I—I don't like the mist."

"We can't lose our way along the riverbank even in this. Don't worry your head about the mist. Just bide still a minute while I get my rod, then we'll get away back."

He turned downriver, and before he had gone ten yards, was swallowed in the mist. I stubbed out my cigarette on the now chilly stone, and watched the grey swirl where he had disappeared. The obliterating cloud pressed closer, on heather, on rock, on the chuckling water.

The dipper warned me first. It burst from under the fog, fleeing upstream with a rattle of alarm notes that made my nerves jump and tingle.

Then through the blank wall of the mist there tore a cry. A curse. A thudding, gasping noise, and the sickening sound of a blow. And a sharp yell from Dougal.

"Lassie! Run!"

Then the horrible sound of harsh breath choking, rasping in a crushed throat; another thud; and silence.

Chapter 20

OF COURSE I SCREAMED. The sound was like a bright knife of panic, slashing at the mist. But the grey swirls deadened it; then they were all round me, clawing and fingering at me, as I stumbled forward towards where Dougal's voice had been.

I am not brave. I was horribly frightened, with a chill and nauseating terror. But I don't think anybody normal would unhesitatingly run *away* if they heard a friend being attacked nearby.

So I leaped forward, only to falter and trip before I had gone five yards, so blinding now was the mist that shrouded the moor. Even the edge of the river was invisible, and a hasty step could result in a broken ankle, or, at best, a plunge into the rock-ridden swirl of waters. I put out my hands, foolishly, gropingly, as if they could pull aside the pale blanket of the mist. I plunged another four yards into it, then I stepped on nothing, and went hurtling down a bank to land on my knees in deep heather.

It was only then that I noticed how complete was the silence. The sounds of the struggle had ceased. Even the river, cut off from me by the bank, ran muted under the mist. I crouched there, shaken and terrified, clutching the wet heather stems, and straining with wide, blind eyes into the blankness around me. I found I was turning my head from side to side with a blind weaving motion, like a new-born beast scenting the air. The mist pressed close, the bewildering, sense-blotting nothingness of the mist, so that I no longer knew which way the river ran, or where I had heard the men fighting, or—where the murderer might, now, be supposed to be.

Then I heard him breathing.

There was a soft step; another. Water spattered off the heather; the stiff sedge rustled, and was still. Silence.

He had been ahead of me, to the right. Of that I was certain, but how near . . .?

The breathing surely came from behind me now. My head jerked round on neck muscles as tight and dry as rope. I could feel my eyes straining wider, my mouth slackening in panic. My hands tightened on the heather stems till I thought he must hear the bones cracking.

And now the breathing had stopped. Somewhere, the river poured its unheeding waters along under the peat banks. Behind me? Before? To the right? I found I could no longer trust my senses, and on the heels of that betrayal panic came.

All at once the mist was full of noises. The rustle of heather was the murderer's breathing, the thud of my own frightened heart his footstep; the surging of blood in my temples blended with the rush of the invisible river, eddying, wavering, distorted by the dizzying mist into the very stuff of terror. . . .

There was salt on my tongue; blood. My lip throbbed painfully where I had bitten it, but the pain had checked the panic. I flattened myself in the long heather, closed my eyes, and listened.

He was there; there had been no illusion about that. He was fairly close, moving towards me, but a little way to one side, between me and the river. I could hear the water now, quite clearly, some few yards away on the right. I went lower in the heather, flat in my form like a hunted animal, glad now of the bewildering mist which was the friend of the hunted more than of the hunter. I had only to keep still; perhaps, when he had passed me, I could break cover and run, and . . .

He was level with me now, between me and the river. His breathing was shallow, rapid, excited. He stopped.

Then, farther away, down along the riverbank, I heard something else. Footsteps, heavy, uncertain footsteps that thudded on heather and then scraped on rock. Dougal Macrae's voice called, thickly: "Lassie . . . lassie, are ye there?"

A great sob of thankfulness tore at my throat, but I choked it back, wondering wildly what to do. If I answered. . . . The murderer was within six yards of me, I knew. I heard his harsh indrawn breath; sensed the tensing of his muscles as he realized that he had failed to eliminate Dougal. If I called to Dougal, was there anything to save my throat from that bright butcher's knife not twenty feet away? A knife which could dispatch me in a matter of seconds, and then turn its dripping point to wait for Dougal to answer my call. . . .

But I must call. . . . Not for help, but for warning. I must cry out, and tell Dougal that he is here, the killer is here, just beside me. *Somehow I must cry out,* and then run, run into the lovely blinding mist, away from the knife and the excited hands of the butcher coming behind me.

And Dougal was coming. He plunged towards us, as bold and heavy as an angry bull. I was on my knees, and my mouth was gaping to shout a warning, when suddenly the murderer turned, and was running upriver like a stag. I could hear him bounding, sure as a deer, through the long heather. And Dougal heard him too. He let out a yell that was a curse, and flung himself after the escaping man. I saw him looming through the fog. I caught the gleam of a blade in his lifted fist, and I saw in his face such a white blaze of anger as to make him unrecognizable. He looked like some avenging giant out of an old myth.

I gasped out something as he plunged past me, but he paid no heed. He brushed by me as if I were not there, and blundered on into the mist after the killer. Even as I cried, in panic: *"Dougal!"* he vanished upriver into the fog. He must have glimpsed or heard his quarry, because my cry was drowned in a harsh eerie yell that startled the sullen heather with its pagan echoes, and sent a flock of oyster catchers screaming up into the mist like witches.

"A mhurtair! A mhich an diabhil! Aie! You bloody murthering bastard! *Aie!"*

One of the birds rocketed over my head with the screech of a damned soul, the mist streaming from its wings in swaths like grey grass under the scythe.

It vanished, and the mist swept down in its wake, and the sound of the men's running was blotted out once more by the muffled silence.

I turned and ran blindly in the opposite direction.

I do not know how long that stumbling terrified flight through the heather lasted. I had succumbed finally to pure panic—mindless, senseless, sobbing panic. I was no longer frightened of the killer. Reason had stayed with me just long enough to show me that he was no longer concerned with me. Attacking an unsuspecting man out of the mist was one thing; facing an armed Highlander, fighting-mad on his own ground, was quite another. No, the murderer had to lose Dougal very effectively in the fog before he dared turn back to me—and then he had to find me.

But panic has nothing to do with reason. Reason, now, had slipped her cogs, and my brain was spinning sickeningly, uselessly, out of control. I ran and jumped and slithered, and the salt tears slid down my face with the wet mist drops, and flickered into my open mouth onto my tongue. The white mist met me like a blank wall; my hands were out like a blind man's; the skin of my face and my palms was wincing as I thrust myself wildly against the intangible barrier. And as I ran I chattered crazily to myself: *"No—oh no—oh no. . . ."*

What brought me up, all standing, with the panic knocked out of me as at the slash of a whip, was the fact that the ground over which I blundered was shaking beneath my feet.

Half-dazedly I peered at the tufted mosses over which I had been running. Tentatively I took another step. The ground shivered, and I backed quickly, only to feel the surface of the moor rocking like the bottom boards of a punt.

I stood very still.

There was a small dreadful sound beneath my feet, as if the ground had sucked in a bubbling breath.

Chapter 21

MY LAPSE FROM REASON had cost me dearly enough. I was well out in the bog of which Roderick had once spoken, and how far out, I had, I found, no idea. Nor could I tell at all accurately from what direction I had been running when I made this last frightening discovery.

Fear flickered its bats' wings at me afresh, but I shook my head sharply, as if by doing so I could drive it away. I stood exactly where I was, trying to ignore the ominous trembling of the earth, and listened for the sound of the river.

But it was of no use. The more I strained my ears, the more confused were the sounds that eddied and swung round me in the mist. I heard, faintly, the muted murmur of flowing water, but it seemed to come from every quarter at once, reflected off the banks of fog, and over it, all the time, whispered and clucked the invisible life of the bog—small lippings, suckings, a million tiny bubbles popping, uneasy breaths. . . .

My feet were sinking. With an almost physical effort, I gathered the last rags of my self-control round me, then stepped quietly towards a tussock of heather a couple of yards away. The feel of its tough, resistant stems under my feet did much to steady my nerves, but my body was shaking uncontrollably now, and my teeth were chattering. I stood islanded on my little tump of heather, peering vainly along the ground in every direction and being met, in every direction, by the same few feet of boggy green, swimming and shifting under the treacherous mist.

But I knew that I must move, must leave my little tuft of safety and go in some direction—any direction. I told myself that the bog was unlikely to be really dangerous, but here, again, reason was no real help. I think it was the fact of being blinded that brought panic pressing so persistently close. If I could have seen even four yards in front of me, seen where my feet were going five steps ahead, it would not have been so bad. But I should be moving blindly over this hideous, shivering bog, ignorant of the real gravity of the danger, and moving, possibly, farther out into a worse place. . . .

I clenched my hands into icy knots, turned in what I imagined to be the direction of the river, and walked slowly forward.

The sheer effort of self-control needed to make me move slowly was so enormous that, mercifully, I could not think about anything else. I wanted to run—dear God, how I wanted to run! But I made myself go slowly, testing each step. Once I trod unwarily on a patch of lighter green, and went up to the knee into black mud. And by the time I had skirted the light patch, stepping warily from one moss hag to the next, I had completely lost all sense of direction again, so that, when a ghostly skeleton shape floated out of the mist beside me, my whole body jerked like a marionette's with fear. It was only the pale ghost of a young birch, a bone-bare branch that lay rotting on the bog—touchwood, crumbling to decay; but in that misty morass it looked solid, and where it lay the tufted reeds were tall and dark and promised safety.

And I drew a breath of hope. The shape that showed so insubstantial through the fog was one I had seen before.

Surely Roderick and I had passed quite near a fallen birch on that first evening's walk? It had lain on our left, not many yards away, between us and the river. I had only to remember which way it had lain in relation to our path, and I could make without delay for the safe ground.

I trod towards it warily, trying to see it again in my mind's eye as I had noticed it the first night. It was quite possibly not the same tree, but in the mind-annihilating swirl of mist even this frail compass was as sure as the pillar of fire in the wilderness. I stood by it, anchored by its deceptive solidity, and tried to remember, steadying myself quite deliberately with hope.

It had been lying, roughly, north and south. Of that I felt sure. And surely I must still be to the river side of it? In which case the safe ground was beyond it, about thirty yards beyond. If I could once reach that, I would, sooner or later, find a sheep track that would lead me down the glen, to within sound of the sea. Or I might find some trickle of running water that would lead me safely to the river and the hotel.

A black shape shot out of the mist at my back, and skimmed, whirring, into invisibility. A grouse. I swore at it under my breath, and quieted my hammering pulses once again. Then I stepped carefully over the birch tree and took what I thought were my bearings, straining my eyes once more against the mist.

It was only then that I became fully conscious of something that had been tugging at the skirts of my senses for a little time. The ground was shaking. I was standing perfectly still, but the ground was shaking.

So complete had been my absorption in my new fear that I had actually forgotten that, somewhere out in the blind world, there was a murderer looking for me with a knife. . . . And here he was, moving steadily across the quaking bog.

I dropped to my face behind the skeleton of the birch. The rushes were thick and tall. Beneath me the ground shivered and breathed. I lay frozen, this time not even frightened, simply frozen, icy, numb. I doubt if even the knife, ripping down through the mist, would have had the power to move me.

"*Gianetta*. . . ." It was a tiny whisper, no more than a harsh breath. It could have been the breathing of the bog, the exhaling of the marsh gas in its million tiny bubbles.

"Gianetta. . . ." It was nearer now. *"Gianetta. . . ."* The mist was rustling with my name. It floated in little dry whispers like falling leaves, swirling lightly down to rest on the shivering ground.

He was moving slowly; under my body I could feel the measured vibrations of his tread. His hands would be out in front of him, groping for me; his whispering probed the silence, reaching out to trap me.

I recognized it, of course. Oh yes, I knew him now, beyond all doubt. I knew now that my unhappy guessing had been right enough; knew now why the Inspector had pitied me; and why Alastair, two nights ago, had given me that look of unexpressed compassion.

"Gianetta. . . ." There it was again, that name—the name that no one else ever called me . . . the name I had heard shouted through the darkness beside Ronald Beagle's funeral pyre. . . . His voice floated down through the mist, a little fainter now, as if he had turned his head away. *"Gianetta,* where are you? In God's name, *where are you?"*

Roderick had guessed, too, of course. I wondered, pressing my body closer to the wet ground, why he had been so sure that I, alone of all the people at Camasunary, would be unharmed.

"Are you there, Gianetta? *Don't be afraid. . . ."*

I don't think I was afraid, now that I knew for certain it was Nicholas. It wasn't that I believed, with Roderick, that, because of the past, Nicholas would never hurt me. It was just that, as that terrible whispering brought my suspicions to life and made them into truth, I didn't care any more. Not about anything.

"Gianetta . . . Gianetta . . . Gianetta. . . ." The syllables pattered down through the mist in fantastic muttered counterpoint. I put my cold cheek down on the soggy grasses, and cried silently, while the fog wavered and whispered with my name, and its ghostly grey fingers pressed me into the marsh.

And then he was gone. The groping voice had faded, echoed and faded again. The quaking of the bog had ceased. A bird had slipped silently and unalarmed across the grass. He was gone.

I got up stiffly, and, myself moving like a weary ghost, trudged uncaring, heedless, mindless, across the bog, away from the last mocking echo of his voice.

And almost at once I was on firm ground, among stones and long heather. I quickened my pace instinctively. The ground was rising steadily away from the bog, and presently I found the mist was wavering and dwindling round me. I plunged up the slope at an increasing rate as my range of vision extended. The fog thinned, shrank, and ebbed away behind me.

As suddenly as a swimmer diving up through the foam of a wave to meet the air, I burst out of the last swirl of mist into the vivid sunshine.

Chapter 22

THE RELIEF WAS SO COLOSSAL, the chance so unbelievable, that I could only stand, blinking, in the clear light of the afternoon sun. My eyes blinded with mist, and still dazzled with crying, took several seconds to get used to the flood of light. Then I saw where I was. I had clambered a little way up the lower slope of Blaven, at a point where a great dyke of rocks bisected the scree, a wall laid uphill like an enormous buttress against the upper cliffs.

The foot of this buttress was lipped by the fog, which held the lower ground still invisible under its pale tide. The glen itself, the loch, the long Atlantic bay, all lay hidden, drowned under the mist which stretched like a still white lake from Blaven to Sgurr na Stri, from Garsven to Marsco. And out of it, on every hand, the mountains rose, blue and purple and golden-green in the sunlight, swimming above the vaporous sea like fabulous islands. Below, blind terror might grope still in the choking grey; here above, where I stood, was a new and golden world. I might have been alone in the dawn of time, watching the first mountains rear themselves out of the clouds of chaos. . . .

But I was not alone.

Hardly had my eyes adjusted themselves to the brilliant spaciousness of my new world above the clouds, when I became aware of someone about fifty yards away. He had not seen me, but was standing near the foot of the rock buttress, gazing past it, away from me, towards the open horizon of the southwest. It was Roderick Grant. I could see the dark-gold gleam of his hair in the sunlight.

I called: "Roderick!" and was amazed at the harsh croak that my stiff throat produced.

He did not move. My knees were shaking, and it was with difficult, uncertain steps that I made my way towards him over the rough ground.

I said his name again: "Roderick!"

He heard then. He swung round. He said: "Yes?" and then: *"Janet!"* His voice sounded raw with shock, but at that I could hardly feel surprised. God knows what I looked like, death-white and shaking, wet and filthy, with the ghosts of terror and despair still looking out of my eyes.

He took two swift strides to meet me, and caught hold of my hands, or I would have fallen. He thrust me down onto a flat rock with my back against the warm stone of the buttress. I shut my eyes, and the sunlight beat against the lids in swirls of red and gold and violet. I could feel its heat washing over me in great reviving waves, and I relaxed in it, drawing my breath more smoothly. Then at length I opened my eyes and looked up at Roderick.

He was standing in front of me, watching me, and in those blue eyes I saw, again, that dreadful look of compassion. I knew what it meant, now, and I could not meet it. I looked away from him, and busied myself pulling off my sodden shoes and unfastening my coat, which slid off my shoulders to lie in a wet huddle on the rock. My blouse was hardly damp, and the grateful heat poured through it onto my shoulders.

He spoke then: "You don't—know?"

I nodded.

He said slowly, an odd note in his voice: "I told you that you would not be hurt. I shouldn't have said it. It was—"

"It hardly matters," I said, wearily. "Though why you thought, after what Nicholas put me through when we got divorced, that he'd have any scruples about me now, I don't know." My left hand was flat on the hot rock. The line where my wedding ring had been showed clear and white on the third finger. I said, still with the weight of dreariness pressing on me: "It was wrong of me to try to protect him, suspecting what he was. I see that now. One shouldn't really put people before principles. Not when the people are—outlaws."

My voice dwindled and stopped. He had turned away from me, and his eyes were on the distant peaks of the Cuillin, where they swam above the vaporous lake.

"Why did you do it?"

I blinked stupidly. "Why did I do what?"

"Protect—him." There was a curious light tone to his voice that might have been relief.

I hesitated, then said flatly: "Because I'm his wife."

He turned his head sharply. "Divorced."

"Oh yes. But—but that made no difference to some things. I mean, one has loyalties—"

He said harshly: "Loyalties? Why call it loyalty when you mean love?"

I said nothing.

"Don't you?"

"I suppose so."

He was silent. Then he said abruptly: "What happened down there? How did you find out?"

"He was looking for me in the mist. He called me. I knew his voice."

"He *called* you! But surely—"

"I was with Dougal Macrae, fishing, when the mist came down. Dougal had gone to get his rod. I heard a struggle, and Dougal must have been knocked out, then he—Nicholas—started looking for me. Only, Dougal recovered and went after him. They both chased off into the mist, and I ran away, but I got lost. And then—and then—"

"Yes?"

"I heard him coming across the bog, calling for me. Not calling, really, only whispering. I suppose he'd given Dougal the slip, and had doubled back to look for me. And he daren't call loudly in case Dougal heard him."

"He must have known that you've guessed who—what —he is."

I shivered a little. "Yes."

He was peering down now at the thick pall that covered the valley. "So Drury is down there. In that?"

"Yes."

"How far away?"

"I don't know. I suppose it was only a few minutes ago that—"

He swung round on me, so suddenly that I was startled.

"Come on," he said, abruptly, almost roughly. "We've got to get out of this. Get your shoes."

He had hold of my wrist, and pulled me to my feet.

"Down into that?" I said, doubtfully. "Shouldn't we wait till it clears a little? He's got—"

"Down? Of course not. We're going up."

"What on earth d'you mean?"

He laughed, almost gaily. *"I will lift up mine eyes unto the hills. . . ."* He seized my coat where it lay on the rock, and shook out its damp folds. Something tinkled sharply onto a boulder, and rolled aside with a glint. "Don't ask questions, Janet. Do as I say. What's that?"

"Oh!" I cried, stooping after it. "It's Heather's brooch!"

"Heather's brooch?" His tone was casual, so casual that I looked at him in some surprise.

"Yes. I found it yesterday under that dreadful ledge. I thought it was Roberta's, but Dougal said—"

Once again my voice dwindled and died in my throat. I stood up, the brooch in my hand, and looked up into his eyes.

I said: "The first night I was here, you told me about Heather's murder. You told me about the little pile of jewelry that was found on the ledge. A bracelet, you said, and a brooch, and—oh, other things. But the brooch *wasn't* on the ledge when she was found. And since she had only been given it that day, for her birthday, you couldn't have known about it, *unless you saw her wearing it yourself. Unless you, yourself, put it onto that little pile on the ledge beside the bonfire."*

High up, somewhere, a lark was singing. Round us, serene above the mist, the mountains swam. Roderick Grant smiled down at me, his blue eyes very bright.

"Yes," he said gently. "Of course. But what a pity you remembered, isn't it?"

Chapter 23

SO WE FACED EACH OTHER, the murderer and I, marooned together on our island Ararat above the flood of cloud;

alone together, above the silent world, on the mountain where already he had sent three people to their deaths.

He was smiling still, and I saw in his face again the look of compassion that, now, I understood. He liked me, and he was going to kill me. He was sorry, but he was going to kill me.

But, just for a moment, even this knowledge was crowded out by the one glorious surge of elation that swept through me. The whole of that silent, cloud-top world was drenched with the light of the sun and the song of the lark—and the knowledge that I had been criminally, stupidly, cruelly wrong about Nicholas. I think that for two full minutes I stared into Roderick Grant's mad blue eyes and thought, not: "I am here alone with a maniac killer," but: "It was not Nicholas, *it was not Nicholas. . . .*"

Roderick said, regretfully. "I'm so sorry, Janet. I really am, you know. I knew when I heard you talking to Dougal by the river, that sooner or later you'd remember. I didn't really mean to, but of course I'll have to kill you now."

I found to my surprise that my voice was quite calm. I said: "It won't help you if you do, Roderick. The Inspector knows."

He frowned. "I don't believe you."

"He told me so. He said he was just waiting for information from London to confirm what he knew. And of course there's Roberta."

His face darkened. "Yes. Roberta."

The vivid eyes hooded themselves as he brooded over his failure with Roberta. I wondered if he had killed Dougal, or if Dougal, with Nicholas, were still hunting through the mist below us . . . the lovely safe mist, not many yards below us.

"Don't try and run away," said Roderick. "I'd only have to bring you back. And don't scream, Janet, because then I'd have to throttle you, and"—he smiled gently at me—"I always cut their throats, if I can. It's the best way."

I backed against the cliff of the buttress. It was warm and solid, and there were tiny tufts of saxifrage in the clefts under my fingers. Real. Normal. I forced my stiff lips to smile back at Roderick. At all costs, I must try to keep him talking. Keep him in this mad, gentle mood. I must speak smoothly and calmly. If I should panic again, my fear might be the spark that would touch off the crazy train of his murderer's mind.

So I smiled. "Why do you do it at all, Roderick? Why did you kill Heather Macrae?"

He looked at me in surprise. "They wanted it."

"They?"

"The mountains." He made an oddly beautiful gesture. "All these years, these ages, they've waited, dreaming like this, above the clouds, watching over the green life of the valleys. Once, long ago, men paid them worship, lit fires for them, gave them the yearly sacrifice of life, but now"—his voice had an absent, brooding tone—"now they have to take for themselves what they can. A life a year, that's what they need . . . blood and fire, and the May-day sacrifices that men paid them when the world was young and simple, and men knew the gods that lived on the mountains."

He looked at me. It was uncanny and horrible, to look at someone's familiar face, to listen to someone's familiar voice, and to see a complete stranger looking out of his eyes.

"She helped me carry the wood and the peat. Together we collected the nine woods and the wild agaric and the oak to make the wildfire. She made the fire for me, and then I cut her throat and—"

I had to stop him. I said abruptly: "But why did you kill Marion Bradford?"

His face darkened with anger. "Those two women! You heard the little one—Roberta—that night. You heard her talking sacrilege, you heard how she chattered of conquering—*conquering*—these." Again the flowing gesture that embraced the dreaming peaks. "And the other one— Miss Bradford—she was the same." He laughed suddenly, and sounded all at once perfectly normal and charming. "It was quite easy. The elder one, that dreadful, stupid woman, she was a little in love with me, I think. She was pleased and flattered when I met them on the mountain and offered to show her the climb across the Sputan Dhu."

"I suppose you thought they were both dead when you left them."

"They should have been," he said. "Wasn't it bad luck?"

"Very," I said drily. My eyes went past him, scanning the fringes of the mist. No one. Nothing.

He was frowning at a sprig of heather that he had pulled. "That ledge where you found Roberta," he said. "I'd been along the damned thing three times already, but I never went farther than the corner when I saw the ledge was empty. I wanted to find her first, of course."

"Of course." The lark had stopped singing. There was no sound in the blue-and-gold day but the grotesque exchange of our pleasant, polite voices, talking about murder.

"But *you* found her." The cock of his eyebrow was almost whimsical. "And you nearly—oh so nearly—gave me the chance I wanted, Janet."

I forgot about being calm and quiet. I cried out: "When you sent me to get the flask! You were going to kill her then!"

He nodded. "I was going to kill her then. A little pressure on the throat, and—" This time the gesture was horrible. "But you came back, Janet."

I licked my lips. "When she opened her eyes," I said hoarsely, "it was *you* she saw. *You*, standing behind me."

"Of course." He laughed. "You thought it was Drury, didn't you? Just as you thought it was Drury who killed Ronald Beagle—"

"Why did you do that?"

He hesitated, and into the blue eyes came a look of naïve surprise. "D'you know, I don't quite know, Janet. I'd hated him for a long time, of course, because I knew that to his mind *they* were just so many peaks to be climbed, so many names to be recorded. And then he came among us that night, on the mountain, talking so glibly of Everest—Everest conquered, those untouchable snows defiled and trampled, where I had thought no man could ever put his sacrilegious feet . . . *You* said that, Janet. You remember? You spoke like that about it once, and, because of that, I thought that I could never hurt you. . . . But Beagle—I followed him down the hill. I caught him from behind and killed him." His eyes met mine ingenuously. "I think," he said, "I must have been a little mad."

I said nothing. I was watching the edge of the mist, where it frothed along the empty mountainside.

"And now," said Roderick, feeling in his coat pocket, "where's my knife?" He patted his coat carefully, as a man does when he is wondering where he has put his pipe. The sun gleamed on his dark-gold hair. "It doesn't seem to be—oh yes, I remember now. I was sharpening it. I put it down somewhere. . ." He smiled at me, then he turned and scanned the heather anxiously. "Can you see it, Janet, my dear?"

Little bubbles of hysteria rose in my throat. My fingers dug and scraped at the rock behind me. I stiffened myself with a jerk and flung out an arm, pointing at the ground beyond him.

"There, Roderick! There it is!"

He swung round, peering

I couldn't get past him, down into the mist. I had to go up.

I went up the end of that buttress like a cat, like a lizard, finding holds where no holds were, gripping the rough rock with stockinged feet and fingers which seemed endowed with miraculous, prehensile strength.

I heard him shout *"Janet!"* and the sound acted like the crack of a whip on a bolting horse. I went up ten feet of rock in one incredible, swarming scramble, to haul myself, spread-eagled, onto the flat crest of the buttress.

The enormous wing of rock soared in front of me up to the high crags. Its top was, perhaps, eight feet wide, and strode upwards at a dizzy angle, in giant steps and serrations, like an enormous ruined staircase. I had landed, somehow, on the lowest tread, and I flung myself frantically at the face of the next step, just as the ring of boots on rock told me that he had started after me.

How I got up what seemed to be twenty feet of perpendicular rock, I do not know. But my mad impetus still drove me, holding me against the cliff, clamping my hands instinctively into crannies, bracing my feet against juts of safe rock, propelling me upwards as thoughtlessly and as safely as if I were a fly walking up a wall.

With a heave and a jerk I dragged myself onto the wider ledge that marked the second step. And, inexorably, the next perpendicular barred my way, this time gashed from summit to foot by a vertical crack, or chimney. I flew at this, only to be brought up short as I saw that the rock on which I stood was a stack, a chunk split off the main buttress, and between me and the next upright there yawned a gap which dropped sheer away to the level of the scree.

The gap was perhaps four feet wide, no more. And at

the other side, on one wall of the chimney was a smallish, triangular ledge, above which a deep crevice held a slash of shadow.

There was my handhold, there the ledge for my feet, if I could only get across that dreadful gap. . . . But I was nearly foundered, and I knew it. My breath was coming in painful gasps; I had knocked one of my feet; my hands were bleeding.

I hesitated there, on the brink of the split in the rock. Then I heard the rattle of pebbles behind me—close behind. I turned, a terrified thing at bay, my eyes desperately searching for another way off the top of the stack. To left, to right, a sheer drop of thirty feet to the scree. Before me, the chasm. A hand swung up over the edge of the platform where I stood. A dark-gold head rose after it. Mad blue eyes, rinsed of all humanity, stared into mine.

I turned and leaped the gap without a second's thought. I landed on the little ledge. My knee bumped rock, but I hardly felt it as my hands, clawling wildly, found a safe anchorage in the crevice above. Then my knee was in the crevice. With a heave and a wriggle I pulled my body up to it, and was in the chimney, which was narrow enough to let me wedge myself against one side of it while I sought for holds in the other. I swarmed up it like a chimney boy whose master had lit a fire beneath him.

Then my hand slid into a deep grip; I braced myself and with one last heave, one final convulsion, dragged myself out of the chimney and onto a deep ledge sheltered by an overhang.

And this time I was cornered. I knew it. Even if I could have climbed the overhang that bulged above me, the impulse had given out; nature had swung back on me. I was finished. And the place where I now found myself was no more than a ledge of rock, some four feet by ten, piled with small boulders and blazing with bell heather.

I crouched among the scented flowers and peered down. Roderick was standing twenty feet below me at the edge of the gap, his convulsed face lifted to mine. His breathing was ragged and horrible. I saw the sweat gleaming on his flushed cheekbones, and on the knuckles of the hand in which he held the knife. . . .

I screamed then. The sound splintered against the rocks into a million jarring, tearing echoes that ripped the silence of the afternoon into tatters. The raven swept out from high above me with a frightened bark.

Something flashed past my cheek with the whistle of a whiplash. The wind of it seared my face. Roderick's knife struck the cliff behind me, and shattered into a hundred little tinkling notes that were whirled into the bellow of the echo as I screamed again.

The empty rock flung my terror back at me, hollow, reverberating. The raven swung up, yelling, into the empty blue air. Away to the west, in the greater emptiness, the Cuillin dreamed on indifferently. I crouched in my eyrie high above the sea of cloud, an insignificant insect clinging to a crack in a wall.

Roderick swore harshly below me, and his now empty hands lifted, the fingers crooked like claws.

"I'm coming up," he said on a savage, breathless note, and I saw his knees flex for the leap across the gap.

My fingers scrabbled at the heather, caught up a big jagged rock, and held it poised on the brink of the ledge.

"Keep off!" My voice was a croak. "Stay where you are, or I'll smash your head in!"

He glanced up again, and I saw him recoil half a pace. Then he laughed, and with the laugh the whole situation split up, and re-formed into a yet crazier pattern, for the laughter was genuine and full of amusement. From the face he lifted to me, all the savagery had been wiped clean; it held the familiar gaiety and charm, and—yes, affection.

He said ruefully: "I broke my knife, Janet. Let me come up."

I held onto the rags of my own sanity. "*No!* Stay where you are or I'll throw this down on you!"

He shook the hair out of his eyes. "You wouldn't do a thing like that, Janet darling," he said, and leaped the gap like a deer.

Then he was standing on the little triangular ledge below me, one hand locked in the crevice. I saw his muscles tense as he prepared to heave himself up the chimney after me.

His head was back; his blue eyes held mine.

"You couldn't do a thing like that, could you?" he said.

And, God help me, I couldn't. My fingers clutched the jagged boulder. I lifted it, ready to heave it down . . . but something held me—the imagined impact of rock on flesh, the smashing of bone and eyes and hair into a splintered nothing . . . I couldn't do it. I turned sick and dizzy, and the rock slipped from my hands back onto the ledge among the flowers.

"No," I said, and I put out both my hands as if to ward off the sight of the violence I could not do. "No—I can't. . . ."

He laughed again, and I saw the knuckles of his left hand whiten for the upward pull. Then something smashed into the rock not six inches from his head. The report of the gun slammed against the echoing mountain with a roar like an express bursting from a tunnel.

"Don't worry, Gianetta, I can," said Nicholas grimly, and fired again.

Chapter 24

ONLY THEN DID I BECOME AWARE that, a little way to the north, the edge of the mist was broken and swirling at last, as men thrust out of it and began to race along the hillside: the Inspector, Hecky, Neill, and Jamesy Farlane, all making at the double for the foot of the stack.

Nicholas, well ahead of them, had already reached the base of the buttress. The slam of his second shot tore the echoes apart, and now the rock by Roderick's hand splintered into fragments. I heard the whine of the ricocheting bullet, and I saw Roderick flinch and, momentarily, freeze against the rock.

The other men, running at a dangerous pace along the scree, had almost come up with Nicholas. I heard the Inspector shout something.

Roderick half turned on his little ledge, braced himself for an instant, then flung himself, from a stand, back across the gap between the ledge and the stack. The nails of his boots ripped screaming along the rocky platform, then they gripped. In the same moment I heard the scrape and clink of boots as the pursuers, spreading out, started to climb the north face of the buttress.

Roderick paused for an instant, balanced, as it were, in mid-flight on the top of the stack. The sun glinted on his

gold hair as he glanced quickly this way, that way. . . .
Then he leaped for the south side of the stack, swung himself over, and disappeared from view.

Someone yelled. Hecky was half up a lower step of the buttress, and had seen him. I saw him cling and point, shouting, before he addressed himself even more desperately to the cliff.

But Roderick had a good start, and he climbed like a chamois. In less time than it takes to tell, I saw him dart out onto the scree south of the buttress, and turn downhill. He was making for the mist, with that swift leaping stride of his, and I heard the Inspector curse as he, too, started to run downhill.

But Nicholas had moved faster. He must have heard Roderick jump down onto the scree, for only a few seconds after he began his dash for the shelter of the mist, Nicholas had turned and started down the north side of the buttress.

From my dizzy eyrie, I could see them both. To that incredible day, the race provided as fantastic a climax as could well be imagined. There was the great dike, swooping down the side of the mountain, to lose itself in the sea of fog; and there, on either side of it, ran hunter and hunted, law and outlaw, slithering, leaping, glissading down the breakneck scree in a last mad duel of speed.

Once, Roderick slipped, and fell to one knee, saving himself with his hands. Nicholas gained four long strides before he was up again and hurtling downhill, unhurt, to gain the shelter of the mist. Not far to go now . . . thirty yards, twenty . . . the buttress had dwindled between them to a ridge, a low wall . . . then Roderick saw Nicholas, and swerved, heading for safety at an angle away from him.

I saw Nicholas thrust out a foot, and brake to slithering ski turn in a flurry of loose shale. Something gleamed in his hand.

The Inspector's yell came from somewhere out of sight below me. *"Don't use that gun!"*

The gun flashed down into the heather as Nicholas put a hand to the low dike and vaulted it. Roderick gave one quick glance over his shoulder, and in three great bounds reached the margin of the mist. It swirled and broke around his bolting form, then swallowed him into invisibility.

Twenty seconds later the same patch swayed and broke as Nicholas thrust into it, and vanished.

Then, all around me, the cliffs and the clear blue air swung and swayed, dissolving like the mist itself. The scent of the heather enveloped me, sickening-sweet as the fumes of ether, and the sunlight whirled into a million spinning flecks of light, a vortex into which, helpless, I was being sucked. An eddy, a whirlpool . . . and I was in it. I was as light as a cork, as light as a feather, as insubstantial as blown dust. . . .

Then out of the spinning chaos came Inspector Mackenzie's voice, calm, matter-of-fact, and quite near at hand.

He said: "Wake up, lassie, it's time we got you down from there."

I found that my hands were pressed to my eyes. I took them away, and the boiling light slowly cleared. The world swung back into place, and I looked down.

Inspector Mackenize was on the top of the stack, standing where Roderick had stood, and Jamesy Farlane was with him. "How in the world did you get up there, anyway?"

I don't remember," I said truthfully. I sat there on my cushion of heather and looked down at the two men, feeling suddenly absurd. "I—I can't get down, Inspector."

He was brisk. "Well, lassie, you'll have to be fetched. Stay where you are." The pair of them became busy with ropes, and then Jamesy approached my cliff. He got across the gap with ludicrous ease, and paused there, examining the chimney.

The Inspector, I saw, was looking back over his shoulder.

"Nicholas—" I said hoarsely, but he cut me short.

"Hoots awa' wi' ye"—it was the one conventionally Scottish expression that I ever heard him use—"don't worry about that. Hecky and Neill both went after him, as you'd have seen if you hadn't been so busy fainting. Your man's safe enough, my dear."

And, even he finished speaking, I saw Nicholas come slowly up out of the mist. He moved stiffly, like a very tired man, but he seemed to be unhurt. He raised his head and looked up towards us, then quickened his pace, lifting a hand in some sort of gesture which I could not interpret, but which seemed to satisfy the Inspector, for he grunted, and gave a little nod as he turned back to watch Jamesy's progress.

I cannot pretend that I was anything but an appalling

nuisance to poor Jamesy, when at last he appeared beside me on the ledge with a rope, and attempted to show me how to descend from my eyrie. In fact, I can't now remember how this descent was eventually accomplished. I remember his tying the rope round me, and passing it round his own body, and round a spike of rock; I also remember a calming flood of instructions being poured over my head as I started my climb, but whether I obeyed them or not I have no idea. I suspect not; in fact, I think that for the main part of the descent he had to lower me, helplessly swinging, on the end of the rope. And since I could not possibly have jumped the gap to the stack, Jamesy lowered me straight down the other thirty feet or so into the bottom of the cleft itself. I remember the sudden chill that struck me as I passed from the sunlit chimney into the shadow of the narrow gully.

Then my feet touched the scree, and, at the same moment, someone took hold of me, and held me hard.

I said: "Oh, Nicholas—" and everything slid away from me again into a spinning, sun-shot oblivion.

Chapter 25

WHEN NICHOLAS DIVED into the pool of mist after Roderick, he was not much more than twenty yards behind him, and, though the mist was still thick enough to be blinding, he could hear the noise of his flight quite distinctly. It is probable that Roderick still believed Nicholas to have a gun, while he himself, having lost his knife, was unarmed; he may, too, have heard Neill and Hecky thudding down the hillside in Nicholas's wake; or he may, simply, have given way at last to panic and, once running, have been unable to stop—at any rate, he made no attempt to attack the pursuer, but fled ahead of him through the fog, until at length they reached the level turf of the glen.

Here going was easier, but soon Nicholas realized he was rapidly overhauling his quarry. Roderick, it will be remembered, had already had to exert himself considerably that afternoon, and now he flagged quickly; the panic impulse gave out and robbed him of momentum. Nicholas was closing in, fifteen yards, ten, seven...as the gap closed, panic supervened again, and Roderick turned and sprang at his pursuer out of the fog.

It was a sharp, nasty little struggle, no holds barred. It was also not quite equal, for whereas Nicholas had only, so to speak, a mandate to stop the murderer getting away, the murderer wanted quite simply to kill his pursuer if possible. How it would have ended is hard to guess, but Neill and Hecky, guided by the sounds of the struggle, arrived in a very short time, and Roderick, fighting literally like a madman, was overpowered. And when Dougal Macrae, still breathing fire and slaughter, suddenly materialized out of the fog as well, the thing was over. Roderick, unresisting now, was taken by the three men back to the hotel, where he would be held until transport arrived. Nicholas, breathing hard, and dabbing at a cut on his cheek, watched the mist close round them, then he turned and made his way back up the hillside into the sun.

So much I had learned, sitting beside Nicholas on the heather at the foot of the buttress, with my back against its warm flank. I had been fortified with whisky and a cigarette, and was content, for the moment, to rest there in the sun before attempting the tramp back to the hotel.

The Inspector, it appeared, was to set off immediately with his prisoner for Inverness. He paused before us as he turned to go.

"Are you sure you're all right, lassie?"

"Quite, thank you," I said, and smiled at him through the smoke of my cigarette.

He glanced from me to Nicholas, and back again. "It seems I was wrong," he said drily.

"What d'you mean?"

"In thinking you were withholding evidence that mattered."

I felt myself flushing. "What did you imagine I knew that I hadn't told you?"

"I thought you'd recognized the man you saw in front of the bonfire."

"Oh. No, I hadn't. I hadn't, really."

"I believe you. . . ." But his glance was speculative and I felt the flush deepen. "Even so, I could almost have sworn you were lying just then about something."

"I was," I said, "but not about that. It was something I heard, not something I saw."

His gaze flicked to Nicholas once more, and he smiled. "Ah," he said. "Just so. Well, I'll be away. I'm glad to be leaving you in such good hands. Take care of her, sir. She's had a rough time."

"I will," said Nicholas.

"One thing"—Inspector Mackenzie regarded him with some severity—"you have, of course, got a license for your gun?"

"Gun?" said Nicholas, blankly. "What gun?"

The Inspector nodded. "I thought as much," he said drily. "Well, see you get one."

And, with another nod, he turned and was presently swallowed up in the mist.

And we were alone on the mountainside, islanded in the pool of mist, where, on every hand in the golden distance, the mountaintops drifted, drowsing in their own halcyon dreams. Sweet and pungent, the honey smells of rockrose and heather thickened round us in the heat, and, once more, the lark launched himself into the upper sky, on a wake of bubble-silver song.

I drew a little sigh, and settled my shoulders gratefully against the warm rock.

"It's all over," I said. "I can hardly believe it, but it's all over."

"My God, but you had me worried!" said Nicholas. "I knew Grant had gone out, but the Inspector had put Neill on to watch him, and then when the mist dropped like that, all in a moment, and Neill came back and said he'd lost his man. . . ." He glanced briefly down at me. "I knew where you and Dougal were fishing, so I made upriver as fast as I could. The police turned straight out after Grant. Then I heard a yell from Dougal, and you screamed, and I ran like blazes. I found your fishing rods, but you'd gone, so I started hunting you. I went across the bog—"

"I know. I heard you. I was hiding quite near."

"Silly little devil."

"Well, I was scared. I thought you were the murderer—and you didn't help by whispering my name in that blood-curdling way."

He laughed ruefully. "I'm sorry. But I knew Grant might be nearer you than I was, and if you'd called out from too far away he might have reached you first. No, I wanted to get you safe under my wing, and then—"

"So you *knew* it was Roderick."

He glanced down sideways at me. "Then, yes. I'd been wondering about him for quite some time, and so had Inspector Mackenzie, but there was no proof."

"What was the information he was waiting for from London? Or—no, you'd better start at the beginning, Nicholas. Tell me—"

"That *is* the beginning. The information that came today is really the beginning of the story. It concerns Roderick Grant's family. Did you know his father was a minister?"

"He told me a little bit about it. I felt rather sorry for him, a lonely little boy all by himself at the back of the north wind—that was what he called his home."

"It's not a bad description either. I've been through Auchlechtie. It's a tiny hamlet of a dozen cottages in a valley near Bheinn a' Bhùird. The manse, where the Grants lived, was four miles even from the village, up beside the ruins of the old church and its primitive grave-yard. The new church had been built down in the village itself, but the minister's house had no one for neighbor except that little square of turf, walled off from the heather, and filled with crumbling headstones and mounds covered with ivy and brambles and old, split yews deformed by the wind."

"And he told me he lived alone with his father."

"So he did. His mother died when he was born and his grandmother, his father's mother, brought him up till he was nine. Then she died—in an asylum."

"Oh, Nicholas, how dreadful. So his father—his father's family—"

"Exactly. His father had always been the stern, un-bending, austere kind of godly Presbyterian that used to be common in fiction and, possibly, even in fact. In him the —the taint showed itself at first only in an increasing remoteness and austerity, a passionate absorption in his studies of the past which, gradually, took complete possession of him, and became more real than the real life round him—if you can apply the term 'real life' to that tiny hamlet, four miles down the empty glen. The history of the long-dead bones in that long-dead grave-yard became, year by year, the only thing that meant anything to him. And the little boy only mattered as being someone to whom he could pour out his half-learned, half-crank theories about the ancient customs and legends of the Highlands."

"Roderick told me that he learned to worship the mountains," I said. "I never guessed he meant it literally."

"But he did, quite literally. He must have spent a large part of his childhood listening to his father's stories and theories, imbibing his mad, garbled versions of the old folk customs of the North, the sort of half-connected, inaccurate rubbish you said he was telling you today. He must have built, bit by bit in his crazed mind, a new sort of mythology for himself, of which the so-called 'ritual' murder of Heather Macrae was a concrete example; a jumble of facts from books and from his father's researches, half-remembered, distorted bits of folklore that shook together like glass in a kaleidoscope and made a picture of violence that seemed, to a madman's brain, to be quite logical."

"I know. I found some of the bits in *The Golden Bough*."

"Oh yes, my *Golden Bough!* The Inspector told me you had it. I was looking all over the place for it last night. I thought I'd left it in my car."

"I'd taken it to read, quite by accident." I told him about it. He glanced down at me with an enigmatic expression.

"So you handed it to the Inspector. If you'd known it was mine—"

"But I did. There was an envelope in it addressed to you in Daddy's writing. I have it in my pocket."

"Have you indeed?" I could feel his eyes on me still, but I would not meet them. "Why didn't you give that to the Inspector, if you knew the book was mine?"

"I—I don't know."

The lark was descending now, in lovely little curves of sound. "How did Daddy know you were here, anyway?"

"What?" He sounded oddly disconcerted. "Oh, I wrote to him and asked him to lend me his copy of the book. There was no one in my flat, so I couldn't send for my own copy. You see, Grant had made one or two remarks that had made me wonder about him—queer little misstatements and inaccuracies that sounded like half-remembered quotations from Frazer and the older books that were Frazer's sources. And when I saw how some of Frazer's details checked with poor Heather Macrae's May-day sacrifice—"

"May Day?"

"May the thirteenth *is* May Day, according to the old calendar. Ancient lore again, you see. Oh, everything fitted, even though it did so in a queer mad way; so, of course, I showed the book to Inspector Mackenzie."

"You did what?" I exclaimed. "When was this?"

"Last week."

"Then he *knew* the book was yours!"

"Of course."

"Then why—" A memory flashed back at me, of the Inspector's kind, compassionate gaze. "Did he never suspect *you*, Nicholas?"

"He may have done, to begin with, and, of course, even after I turned up the evidence of *The Golden Bough* he may have kept me under suspicion, along with Hubert Hay, since we two, as well as Grant, have made some sort of study of local folklore. But Hay had an alibi—with you—for Marion's murder, while I, if you discount the intolerable possibilities of bluff and double bluff, had indicated my innocence by giving evidence to the police. Which left Grant."

"Then why," I said again, "was the Inspector so—so kind, and so *sorry* for me, this morning? He talked about loyalties, and—"

"And you thought he was warning you that I was guilty? Why should you assume that your loyalty should be directed towards me, Gianetta?"

Abruptly, between one wingbeat and the next, the lark's song ceased. He shut his wings and dropped like a flake of shadow into the heather. I said, stupidly: "D'you mean he thought it was *Roderick* I saw by the bonfire?"

"Of course. He thought you were falling for Roderick Grant. That was my fault, I'm afraid. I'd told him so—on very little evidence except that Grant, in his own way, was quite patently interested in you."

I was stupefied. "You told the Inspector that I was in love with Roderick Grant?"

"I did, more or less. Sorry, Gianetta. Sheer dog-in-the-manger stuff. Jealousy exaggerates, you know."

I let that one pass. After a moment he went on: "The

Inspector could only take my word for it, and when you seemed to be protecting Grant he thought you suspected him yourself, but hesitated to give him away."

"But that's absurd! Of course I was never in love with him! I liked him, yes. I thought he was very charming—but *in love!*" I spoke hotly, indignantly. "It's fantastic nonsense!"

"Why?" The question was bland as cream.

"Why? Because—" I stopped short, and bit my lip. I felt the color flooding my cheeks, and shot a quick glance at him. His eyes, narrowed against the smoke from his cigarette, were fixed dreamily, almost inattentively, on the long glimmering verge of the mist where it lay along the far sea's edge. But there was a smile touching the corner of his mouth. I said hurriedly: "But when did the Inspector finally fix on Roderick? Surely the others at the hotel were suspect too?"

"Of course. Any of the other men—Braine, Corrigan, Persimmon, Beagle, could have had an unconfessed interest in folklore, but Marion's murder, remember, narrowed the field down sharply, since it demanded that the murderer also be an efficient climber. And soon afterwards the only climber of the group—poor Beagle—was murdered too."

"Which leaves us with Roderick again."

"As you say. When the Inspector came over yesterday morning he found Roderick, so to speak, leading the field and hardly anyone else running, but still without a thing that could be pinned on him. Then you found Roberta, and he might have got his proof, but he didn't dare wait much longer for her to open her mouth. He put another hurried call through to London for any information about Grant that they could rake up. He was going to risk pulling him in on suspicion if he got anything from them that could justify him. But nothing came through till this morning."

"The fact that his grandmother had died insane? Was that enough?"

"It wasn't all," said Nicholas soberly. "His father died in a mental home two years ago."

"Oh God," I said.

"Quite enough," said Nicholas grimly, "to warrant his being detained—got somehow out of circulation till Roberta could talk. But it was too late. That damned fog came down like a curtain, and Grant gave Neill the slip, and went out looking for you." His arm, somehow, was round my shoulders. "Bloody little fool," he said angrily, his mouth against my hair.

"I'd have been all right with Dougal if the mist hadn't come down," I said defensively. "Nicholas, tell me something."

"Yes?"

"Dougal—he had a knife. I saw it. Did he—down there when you caught Roderick—he didn't—hurt him?"

His arm tightened, as if in protection. "No," he said soberly. "He came up spitting fire and brimstone and revenge, poor devil, but he shut up as soon as he saw Grant."

"Why?"

"Grant collapsed. When I caught him first, he fought like a wildcat, but when Dougal got there as well, and he saw it was hopeless, he just seemed to deflate. To break. He went suddenly quite helpless and gentle, and —I can't describe it, quite. It was rather beastly. He seemed to change character all in an instant."

"He did it with me."

"Did he? Then you'll know just how unspeakable it was. I'd just hit him on the jaw, and then there he was smiling at me like a nice child, and wiping the blood away."

"Don't think about it, Nicholas. He wouldn't remember you'd just hit him."

"I suppose not. He just smiled at all of us. That was when Dougal put his knife away and took him by the arm and said, 'Come on, laddie. Ye'd best be getting back oot of the fog. . . .' He went quite happily with the three of them." He dragged at his cigarette. "After they'd gone a little way off, into the fog, I heard him singing."

"Singing?" I stared at him.

"Well, crooning a tune, half to himself." His eyes met mine. "'*I to the hills will lift mine eyes, From whence doth come mine aid. . . .*'" He looked away. "Poor devil. Poor crazy devil. . . ."

I said swiftly: "They'll never hang him, Nicholas."

"No."

He ground out his cigarette on a stone, and pitched it away as if with it he could extinguish and discard the memory of that nasty little scene. Then he turned his head again, and his voice changed abruptly.

"You saw me with Marcia Maling, didn't you?"

"Yes."

"I heard you go past us when she—when we were kissing outside her room."

"You heard me? But I hardly made a sound."

He smiled crookedly. "My dear girl, my instincts work overtime where you're concerned. Even in the dark, and when I'm kissing another woman."

"Perhaps even more when you're kissing another woman," I said drily, and got a wry look from him.

"I suppose I deserve that one. But this time, I promise you, I was more kissed against than kissing."

"All night?" I said.

His brows shot up. "What the devil d'you mean?"

I told him how I had heard a man's voice in her room later that night. "So of course I assumed it was you. And when I asked you next morning—"

"I—see. I thought you were just referring to the kiss you'd seen. No, Gianetta, I did not spend the night with her. I merely got—how shall I put it?—momentarily way-laid, through no intention of my own."

"I'm sure you struggled madly."

He grinned, and said nothing.

"I suppose the man in her room was Hartley Corrigan? Oh yes, I *see!* That was why he came home early from fishing that night, and yet Alma Corrigan said he didn't get to bed till three!"

"I think so. And when she realized what had happened she took her lipstick and murdered Marcia's doll with it."

"Poor Alma."

"Yes. Well, it's over for her, too. I rather think they've both had a fright, and they realize that they do matter to each other after all. . . ." He paused for a moment, looking down at me under lowered brows. "And now," he said, in a totally different voice, "shall we talk about us?"

I did not reply. My heart was beating lightly and rapidly somewhere up in my throat, and I could not trust my voice. I could feel his eyes on me again, and when he spoke, he did so slowly and deliberately, as if with some difficulty.

He said: "I'm not going to begin with apologies and

self-abasement, though God knows you have plenty to forgive me for, and God knows, too, why you have apparently forgiven me. I'll say all that to you later on. No, don't speak. Let me finish. . . . What I want to say to you now is quite simple, and it's all that matters in the world to me. I want you back, Gianetta. I do most damnably want you back. I suppose I knew I'd been a fool—a criminal, brutal fool—about two days after you'd gone, and then my pride stepped in and stopped me coming after you."

I remembered how I had told Alma Corrigan that there was no room for pride in marriage. His next words were almost an echo—almost.

He said: "But pride and love won't go together, Gianetta. I discovered that. And I do love you, my darling. I don't think I ever stopped." He took me gently by the shoulders, and turned me so that I had to face him. "Will you have me back, Gianetta? Please?"

"I never did have any pride where you were concerned, Nicholas," I said, and kissed him.

Later—a long time later—he said, rather shakily: "Are you sure? Are you sure, my darling?"

"Quite sure." The words were decided enough, but my voice was uncertain as his. I added, foolishly: "Darling Nicholas."

"Gianetta *mia*. . . ."

Later—a rather longer time later—he held me away from him, and laughed.

"At least, this time, there's no doubting the solid worth of my affections!"

"Why not?"

He looked down at me with the old, mocking look. "If you could see yourself, my Lady Greensleeves, you wouldn't ask me that! And if Hugo were here——"

"Which God forbid——"

"Amen. . . . No, don't try and tidy yourself up. It couldn't be done, and in any case I like you dirty, wet, and semiragged. I want to concentrate on your beautiful soul."

"So I noticed."

He grinned, and his arm tightened round my shoulders.

"It wasn't just coincidence that I met you here, you know."

"Wasn't it? But how——?"

"Your father," he said succinctly.

"D'you mean to tell me—?"

He nodded, still grinning. "I got into touch with your people again some time ago. As you know, the divorce upset them very much, and they were only too anxious to help me put things straight." He smiled down at me. "Poor Gianetta, you didn't stand much chance. Your father told me flatly that you'd never be happy without me, and your mother—well, I don't think she ever has quite grasped the fact that we were divorced, has she?"

"No. For Mother, divorce just doesn't exist."

"That's what I understood. Well, I was here at the beginning of May, and I happened to write to your father from this address, to ask him about *The Golden Bough*. A little later I rang him up—I was at Armadale then— and he told me you were due for a holiday, and that he'd contrived—"

"Contrived!" I said dazedly. I began to laugh. "The— the old Machiavelli! And Mother said it must have been 'meant'!"

"It was meant all right," said Nicholas grimly. "I thought that all I needed was a chance really to talk to you. . . ." He smiled ruefully. "And then you ran away from me and I thought that perhaps your father was wrong and it really was all finished. I'd been so sure . . . I deserved a setdown, by God I did. And I got it. You came—and I couldn't get near you. . . ."

He gave a bitter little laugh. "So of course I behaved just about as badly as I could. I said some pretty filthy things to you, didn't I? I've no excuse, except that I thought I'd go crazy, being so near you, and having no— no claim. Somehow the biggest shock to my egoism was when I found you'd even discarded my name, and my ring."

"I only dropped them when I saw your name in the register. Look." I held out my left hand. The white circle on the third finger stood out sharp and clear against the tan. Nicholas looked at it for a moment, while a muscle twitched at the corner of his mouth, then he turned again and pulled me into his arms. His voice was rough against my hair. "So you're going to let me walk straight back into your life? After what I did? After—"

"You said we'd not talk about that."

"No, I like things made easy, don't I? It would serve

me right if you turned on me now, and told me to get back where I belonged, and stop making a mess of your life."

"No," I said.

The lark had left his nest again, and was bubbling up through the clear air. I touched Nicholas's hand softly. "Just don't—don't ever leave me again, Nicholas. I don't think I could bear it."

His arms tightened. He said, almost with ferocity: "No, Gianetta, never again."

The lark rocked, feather-light, snowflake-light, on the crystal bubbles of his song. The great hills drowsed, drifting head under wing in the luminous haze.

I stirred in his arms and drew a little breath of pure happiness.

"What d'you bet," I said, "that when we arrive at Tench Abbas, Mother'll meet us just as if nothing had ever happened, and serenely show us both into the spare room?"

"Then we'd better be married again before we get there," said Nicholas, "or I won't answer for the consequences."

And so we were.